SUMMER OF HOPE

SUMMER OF HOPE

Rachel had a special reason for taking the job as receptionist in the hairdressers at the end of the High Street. To Boyd Ingram, the hospital's beloved R.M.O there were so many barriers to prevent him getting to know her. Barriers such as the mystery which surrounded the accident in which Rachel's family was killed, and the fact that people called her 'Mrs Roberts'. Where was the husband? How did Dr Thora Benton manage to make such a lovely person as Rachel seem sinister? It needed all Rachel's good nature and courage to break down the barriers.

Summer Of Hope

by

Jill Murray

Dales Large Print Books
Long Preston, North Yorkshire,
BD23 4ND, England.

British Library Cataloguing in Publication Data.

Murray, Jill
    Summer of hope.

    A catalogue record of this book is
    available from the British Library

    ISBN   1-84262-363-X pbk

First published in Great Britain in 1973 by Robert Hale & Co.

Copyright © Jill Murray 1973

Cover illustration © John Hancock by arrangement with
P.W.A. International

The moral right of the author has been asserted

Published in Large Print 2005 by arrangement with
The executor of Jill Murray, care of S Walker Literary Agency

Dales Large Print is an imprint of Library Magna Books Ltd.

Printed and bound in Great Britain by
T.J. (International) Ltd., Cornwall, PL28 8RW

Chapter One

Boyd Ingram straightened up from the patient's bed and smiled warmly at the elderly man who had been watching him so anxiously all the while he had been conducting his examination.

'You're doing well,' he said, with a grasp of the man's shoulder that said far more than the brevity of his words.

Sister covered the man up and left the nurse to tuck in the sheets while she hurried after the two doctors. When alone, Boyd Ingram would have waited for her, talked to her as he proceeded to some other patient. But today Dr Fenton was with him. It was Boyd Ingram that Sister wanted to ask about poor Frank Smithson, not Dr Fenton. Thora Fenton was as unforthcoming to the women staff as an icicle. Not that Boyd Ingram talked very much, but that was because he was shy. Underneath that inarticulate exterior was a heart of gold. Sister North knew it. Everyone knew it.

Dr Thora Fenton, however, was another matter. Anyone but a man – a man like Boyd Ingram moreover – could have seen at a glance that Thora Fenton wasn't really as plain and neat as she appeared to be. She could look quite attractive and paralysingly smart if she wished. She had been something of a fashion plate before Boyd Ingram had come to the hospital.

It was significant that now she wore little or no make-up, had dispensed with her contact lens and wore a business-like pair of dark-framed glasses on the job, and mannish shirts and suits under her white coat. As for Dr Fenton's hair, that couldn't be pulled more tightly into a neater bun than that dark thatch, yet, Sister thought, hurrying after them and waiting for the chance to have a word with Boyd Ingram, she herself distinctly remembered seeing Dr Fenton with a most fantastic hair-do the night of the Hospital Ball, just before Boyd Ingram arrived.

It must be what the young nurses were gossiping about (although heaven knew, Sister North didn't encourage gossip) and that Thora Fenton was out to get poor Boyd Ingram in her clutches. Such a nice man deserved a warm, kinder woman, Sister North thought angrily.

'We'll have a cup of Sister's excellent tea, I think,' Boyd said, standing aside for Sister to go into her office. 'And then I can give her the information she is itching to have,' he said, with a ghost of a twinkle in those tired grey eyes.

Dr Fenton said quickly, 'Oh, no, don't let's bother Sister. Besides, you know what we said we'd do about tea, Boyd.'

And so there was no cosy cup of tea, and milk chocolate biscuits, sitting in Sister North's sunny office, but a quick briefing on Frank Smithson, and hurrying after the impatient Thora, who wanted to go out to tea, at Reynolds' Tea-Rooms.

That was a place Boyd Ingram didn't care for. Thora knew so many people, and he hated the atmosphere of a woman's club. Thora, on the other hand, was shocked at his preference for the hospital canteen and a word with any little nurse who had been working well, or better still, his permanent welcome in the Path Lab with an enamel mug of very good tea with Professor Barnsley. Thora deplored the habits Boyd had, and although she didn't tell him she meant to change them, he sometimes had the feeling that that was what she wanted to do.

Today she moved their relationship one stage further. She always talked 'shop' over tea, in her low, well-modulated voice, but today she showed him, from the window by their table, the hairdressers' where she would be in two hours' time, where he was to pick her up.

'I shall change there, and be all ready, because I'm going to have my hair done

9

specially for the show tonight,' she said, firmly. 'You haven't forgotten, Boyd? Tonight? Dinner and a show?'

He tried not to let the dismay show in his face, but it did. He had forgotten. It wasn't exactly a show they were going to see, either, but a very serious play. He had succumbed in order to get this much-talked-of date over and done with, because his personal and private love was research, and he and Professor Barnsley had a bet on something that Thora wouldn't understand or even approve of. The sort of 'bug' which Professor Barnsley was trying to isolate in a set time was not Thora's idea of polite tea-time conversation nor even of work. She was always saying that a really sensible medical man would go all out for consulting rooms in Harley Street. She told Boyd that with an insistence that puzzled him sometimes. It never occurred to him that it was directed at himself.

Now he looked nervously across the road to where he could just see that window of the hairdressers. 'No, really, Thora, I would much rather not. I can't go into a place like that. I'll wait outside.'

'But you can't park there, that's the whole point, Boyd.' She shook her head at him. 'It isn't one of those places where you get a glimpse of women sitting in a row under the driers. You won't see anything, I promise you! It's rather old-fashioned; it has cubicles. Everyone is decently hidden.'

'No, but I'd much rather not–'

'And you'll be in a dinner jacket and it might be raining so you must wait inside,' she went on. 'It's really all right – Mrs York, the woman who runs it, insists on married women only on her staff, and plain-looking ones they are, too. So you've no need to fear those frightful girls with the terrible eye make-up in Maison Pierre's. It's not like that at all.'

'But–'

'Just go in the door and you'll find a woman sitting at the reception desk. Her name is Mrs Roberts. Tell her you've come for Dr Fenton and she'll just tell you to sit on the chair in the corner while she goes to find me. Now surely that's all right?'

Mrs Roberts. The name had a safe sound about it that he couldn't explain. Not like Pearl or Amanda or Chloe at that other wretched place.

'All right, just this once,' he said, capitulating. 'Now can we discuss Frank Smithson?'

Thora said, 'Of course we can, now that's settled!' and she looked very satisfied. It was one step further in his education. Once he had made that first visit calling for her in the hairdressing salon, she would have him gently prodded along the line of other

11

personal chores, until she had broken him in enough to take him home to meet her family. But that was some way ahead and there was a lot of hard work to be done on him. It had been something of a triumph to persuade him to wear his dinner jacket instead of that hideously casual polo-necked sweater and jacket he usually emerged from the hospital in.

And tonight she would be looking really stylish, with an upswept hair-do that she was used to. He must get used to that, too. No more of this stark masculine business in case he was frightened away by her modern appearance. He must get used to a lot of things she had so far hidden from him.

After they had discussed the cases they were working on together, and finished their tea, he was in a hurry to go. That was a thing she couldn't persuade him to do – linger, because he liked being with her. Other men lingered with her too much. It was Boyd she wanted to do that.

With a small sigh, she got up and followed him out. He was as tall as she liked, and his features weren't bad, though he still had that haggard, unsmiling look. He worked too hard. She was sure it was only out of boredom. She must change that. Persuade him to cultivate a taste in highbrow concerts and card parties with her friends, and then he'd relax. He had good hands, and his shoulders weren't narrow, but he did seem to almost slouch along, as though he didn't care how his clothes hung on him. And he had the name for being such a brilliant doctor! She couldn't think how he could have been neglected for so long.

'Now don't forget,' Thora said briskly, 'Mrs Roberts. Nothing to be nervous about. And park your car in Endell Street – it's handy. The street right facing the hair-dressers. You can watch the car all the time you're waiting for me. I always like to watch my car when I park it in this dump of a town.'

At once Boyd jumped to the defence of Denbarton. 'It's not such a bad town,' he protested, frowning.

'Don't frown, Boyd. You've no idea how forbidding you look when you frown!'

He obligingly stopped frowning, and looked very seriously at her, as if he were thinking thoughts he had no intention of imparting.

'Smile, Dr Ingram,' she teased, and was rewarded by a swift unhappy little smile that had 'duty' bristling all over it. 'Oh, dear,' she said. 'We'll have to think of something really funny to make you laugh. Do you know, I don't think I've ever seen you laugh.'

'Hospital life isn't conducive to laughter,' he told her seriously, and he didn't need to enlighten her as to what he was thinking about just then. The kidney boy they had lost last night.

With a small sigh, she again reminded herself that all this was really worth it, or she wouldn't be struggling so hard. This man was a challenge, one she had arisen to from the first moment she had seen him. A man no woman had been able to do any work on, and there appeared to be many women in that hospital who were trying. Well, she would show all those old fuddy-duddies of doting ward sisters and staff nurses how she could make something of their beloved Dr Ingram!

She thought about him all through her hair appointment. It wasn't her idea of a hairdresser's. She had chosen it because it was rather behind the times, because she knew she would never persuade him to wait for her in the open plan hair salon she had recently abandoned. But the staff here were good of their kind, and the proprietress attentive.

There was one man who did a really good razor cut, and she managed to procure his services. He was her kind. He understood her from the start. His eyes met hers in the mirror and she said quietly, 'The style I have at the moment is strictly for my work. For tonight, however, I want a *real* style. Let yourself go.'

Raoul let himself go, and thoroughly

satisfied her with the result. He was really too good for a little local place in the High Street. Later Thora found out that he was Madame's husband – Will York – though everyone called him Raoul. Having found him, she could settle to think about Boyd Ingram.

Boyd Ingram almost forgot about calling for her. A very interesting case had been brought in from the High Street. The boy had been knocked down, but Boyd's sharp eyes discovered something which lay well beyond the fractured leg. He had him admitted and at once telephoned the professor about it. The Professor came over, and they spent an absorbed hour over the boy, until the ward sister reminded Boyd that he should be off duty. She meant (knowing them both) that Dr Fenton would be waiting and fuming. She liked Dr Ingram and didn't want him to have a nasty evening. She had heard Thora Fenton nagging at junior doctors, nurses, anyone who upset her plans. She knew what Thora Fenton was like when she hadn't been treated as she liked to be.

Boyd was put out. 'Oh, bother,' he muttered. 'I tell you what,' he said to Professor Barnsley, 'It's only dinner and some confounded play. I'll see if I can cut out the theatre and slip back. We'll go over this again.'

Professor Barnsley caught the Sister's agonized glance, and shook his head, grinning. 'No, don't do anything so daft. This will keep till tomorrow! We'll have the laddie all comfortable and ready for you, and we'll see what else we can find, eh? Bring Dr Fenton with you,' he added kindly but with reluctance. He loathed Thora Fenton, but like the ward sister, he didn't want his friend to suffer.

Boyd nodded and marched out. He dressed hastily and shot out of Residents, forgetting he was supposed to take his car, in his absorption over this new case. He walked down the narrow street unseeingly, as he ticked off the point they had discovered in his mind. They must have more details of the boy's background. That was the first thing. Heredity could play a big part in that condition. Boyd had almost arrived at the hairdressers' when he remembered he should have brought the car. That was because he had seen 'Endell Street' up on the wall of a house and it rang a bell. Park in Endell Street, Thora had told him.

It was a wide road of solid villas, and this was the quiet end of the High Street, where the shops were beginning to peter out into more houses. He wondered what he ought to do, and decided nervously that he'd better go in and find out how advanced Thora was. If she wasn't ready, he could nip

16

back and she would never need to know how forgetful he'd been.

Mrs Roberts, Thora had said. At the reception desk.

He opened the door and stood there, looking across the intervening space. He wasn't a superstitious man, nor a man who thought very much about significant meetings. Where possible he skipped out of meeting people because small talk bored him and new people (if they were young women) rather scared him. But this meeting was different. A queer little warm glow began to steal over him and for no sensible reason, he was glad he had come. He closed the door behind him in a dazed way and again forgot about Thora.

Mrs Roberts looked up at once, and smiled at him. Not the turned-on artificial smile that he had encountered before from people in hair salons and stores, but one of those radiant smiles that one doesn't want to see turned off. The sort of smile that began at the mouth and lingered long afterwards in the eyes. He hadn't seen that sort of smile since, when? He slowly began to walk towards her, trying to remember, and couldn't. Someone he had seen at home, a long time ago, perhaps in the kitchen, doing comfortable things with food preparation and smiling in natural good nature just because another person had

17

come in sight.

She said, 'Are you Dr Ingram?' which saved him the awful agony of remembering what Thora had told him to say.

He nodded, and didn't know that her smile had called up one of singular sweetness in his own rather tired face.

She said, 'I thought you might be. I saw you in the hospital the other day.'

Hospital … his first and only love. 'I say, did you? Where? Which ward, I mean?'

She was equally enthusiastic. 'The Thomas Gresham Ward. My young sister was in for a check-up.'

'Your sister? What's her name?'

'Deirdre Arden. She lost the use of her legs in an accident. They keep having her in to see why she can't walk, but nothing comes of it.'

'Oh, yes, I remember Deirdre. Pretty little thing with a lot of flaxen hair. Yes. Your sister?' He looked with more attention at Mrs Roberts, who was probably only five years older than the eighteen-year-old Deirdre. Her hair was a light brown, swept severely back, but her eyes were the same deep, intense blue of Deirdre's. He sat down in the nearest chair to her, and started to talk about Deirdre's condition, but the telephone kept ringing, and interrupted what might have been a rather interesting conversation.

Then someone looked out through a slit in

a curtain and Mrs Roberts nodded, while she went on making an appointment and the head vanished. That, he thought, with a sigh, would be someone to report to Thora that he was there.

Mrs Roberts put the telephone down, made her entry in the big book in front of her and asked suddenly where he had parked his car. 'Our road is rather full up today, I'm afraid.'

He started guiltily. 'Oh, I knew there was something I'd forgotten. I suppose I'd better go back for it. Your road?' he asked, thinking of what she had said.

'Yes, Endell Street. Ours is the second house. I can see it from here, where I'm sitting,' Mrs Roberts said, in a pleased sort of way. And then Thora came out.

Some women just look dressed up, but when Thora Fenton was out of her white coat and not pretending to be dowdy for Boyd's benefit, she was splendid. She looked special and she knew it, and she stood, having made her entrance, to see the effect on Boyd Ingram.

He leapt to his feet, but her appearance didn't make much impact because he expected her to be furious because he had forgotten the car. 'I say, Thora, I'm sorry, I forgot the car. Will you wait here while I nip back and get it or shall we walk – oh, no, better not in those clothes,' he said in a bothered way, as he suddenly realized he hadn't seen her looking like this before.

The effect misfired, and Thora saw it. He hadn't expected it, and it put him out. She registered, annoyed, that he didn't like surprises. She had changed and was wearing a shimmering dark dress and plain coat with a matching shimmering border, and shoes that were mainly narrow straps, silver shoes.

There was a momentarily awkward silence, while he wondered what he was expected to say. Mrs Roberts said with her nice smile, but a meaningful tone in her voice for his benefit, 'That's a gorgeous hair style, Dr Fenton. It really suits you. Did Raoul do it?'

Thora Fenton smiled thinly as Boyd, jumping to his cue just a split second too late to be convincing, said, 'Yes, rather, marvellous,' and managed to look abashed at the whole effect.

Thora said, with that thin smile, 'I'm happy to know that Raoul's efforts have met with *your* approval Mrs Roberts.'

If Mrs Roberts noticed the barb, she gave no sign. 'Raoul is Madame's husband,' she said quietly. 'He's the best stylist I know.' It was meant to suggest that only the best had been offered to Dr Fenton, but Thora looked coldly at her and then turned her back. 'Well, Boyd,' she said, 'If you're going to get the car, perhaps you'd better!'

He made good speed back to the Residents' Car Park and didn't have his usual trouble in getting unparked, but Thora was waiting on the kerb for him when he arrived. He tried to see what Mrs Roberts was doing, but the reception desk was empty.

'Why didn't you wait inside?' he asked, but she didn't deign to answer. She was simmering with anger.

She got into the car with care and sat straight-backed until they had left the town. Then she asked sharply, 'How long had you been sitting at the desk talking?'

He took time to answer, concentrating on the traffic. He didn't like driving. Presently, with a little side smile, he murmured, 'Me? *Talking?*' which side-tracked her – it was so apt; so he didn't have to answer the question. But Thora wasn't satisfied. 'Well, so she talked to you. What about?' she persisted.

Diplomacy wasn't his line, but he really rose to it this time, because he didn't want to discuss Mrs Roberts with Thora. 'Why, she talked about you, of course, and how good their establishment was. What did you think she talked about?'

She didn't know, and didn't answer that. She was aware of a wave of jealousy, to think that he could sit comfortably with some other woman, and forget to bring the car for her. She had felt a fool. It wasn't his fault, of course. She blamed that Roberts woman. But she didn't want to upset anyone there;

21

that Raoul was a real find.

It wasn't a very happy evening, although Thora pandered to him and let him talk shop. Somehow tonight, her discussion seemed rather clinically cold. She wasn't, he saw for the first time, really interested in the patients as persons. They were numbers on her round, to be got through, before she left the hospital. He had always thought of her as a good friend who liked talking about their work on the wards, but she made it quite clear that talking 'shop' was not her idea of an evening out. He supposed it had always been like this, but he hadn't noticed it before, and he felt dashed.

'Why are you looking like that Boyd?' she wanted to know. 'I'm one of the sensible ones. You're not. You'll be old before you've been young, worrying over them as you do. That isn't what we were taught to do. It's enough to do the best one can and then put them out of the mind until the next visit.'

He didn't answer, but sat looking at her, stirring his coffee as if he weren't aware of what he was doing.

'Boyd, are you listening to me? Well, say something!'

'All right, I don't agree with what you've just said,' he murmured. 'I didn't want to say it. It sounds discourteous.'

'And I love your old-fashioned courtesy to women,' she said quickly, 'but I could shake you when I see you burning yourself out as you do. You must save yourself for all the other patients that are lining up waiting for your attention over the years, not burn yourself out over the few you see now! Don't you see?'

'I see what you mean,' he allowed at last after a lengthy pause which made her irritation deepen.

'Boyd, how old are you, may I ask?'

'Oh, now let's see,' he said, doing arithmetic.

'Don't you know? Don't your family keep up your birthday?'

This was forbidden ground. So far she had drawn a blank when she had tried to probe into his background. Nobody seemed to know what his background was, although there was a rumour that he was quietly wealthy, beyond the level of his salary, but Thora argued that she had told him so much about her own background that the least he could do was to return the compliment.

'I seem to remember having a thirty-first birthday,' he said, 'and no, I don't get cards or presents from people.' He smiled fleetingly as he said it, and as always with him, that seemed to clinch the matter and close the subject.

She gave it up and let him slide comfortably into a state of listening to her talk, and putting in a word here and there. She always had the feeling when he did that, that he was not really with her but thinking of something else. But tonight he followed the play with some interest. It had a medical background to the plot, which annoyed her and intrigued him – she had wanted to get away from everything to do with the hospital. So long as he didn't want to discuss it all the way back, that would be all right. She wanted him to keep his mind on other things.

'Did you like the play, Boyd?' she asked him as they went out to his car, and he allowed, 'Yes.'

'I did, too,' she told him firmly. 'In fact, it's a long time since the evening went so quickly,' and he said, 'Yes.'

'Where are we going now?' she murmured, as she got into the car beside him.

'Well, back to the hospital, of course,' he said abstractedly. 'Have you seen my gloves, Thora?'

'No. Look for them later, Boyd. Do let's go for a little spin. It's been such a wonderful night.'

He remembered that he had wanted to cut the play but his old friend hadn't wanted him to. There was wisdom in not doing that; Thora would merely have wanted to make another such date fairly soon. The same applied to her present suggestion. He didn't want this sort of thing to be repeated. It was different now, in some way he couldn't define. Before, he had liked Thora's friendship, in preference to lonely hours off duty, because in the past Thora had looked neat and no-nonsense and had talked 'shop'. Tonight it had changed somehow. She was all dressed up, and pressing for the things other people's womenfolk pressed for – a drive in the car, prolonging the evening out, for instance. And she was using perfume, he suddenly realized. Instantly wary, he realized too late that she was just like any other man's woman's friend, and that was just what Boyd himself hadn't wanted.

There was this new wariness in his tone as he said, 'All right, a short run to the coast.'

'Are you always so suspicious in your treatment of your guests for the evening?' Thora teased.

'I expect so,' he said, and she knew he wasn't really considering the matter, because she was well aware that there never were any other guests. It was a matter of extreme irritation to her that if she didn't go further, towards a successful conclusion – engagement and marriage – they would all be amused that she had failed. It was accepted at the hospital that he was in an impregnable bachelor state, which even the prettiest of the staff nurses hadn't been able to alter.

'Don't you think you could make an exception just for once, and forget about the hospital and think about this lovely moonlight night,' she suggested lazily, 'and discuss something else with me?'

'Such as what?' he asked, suspicion deep in his tones now.

'Only about a house I've seen along this stretch of coast,' she said, in surprise. 'What did you think I wanted to discuss?'

'I had no idea, Thora, but then I never do have any idea of what you are going to discuss.'

'Is that good?' she wanted to know.

'Well,' he said carefully, not wanting to offend her, but obviously a little out of his depth, 'it calls forth a certain amount of effort to tidily tuck away the problems of every day and concentrate on what you might be wanting to talk about, because you do each subject so thoroughly. What is so special about the house along this road?' he asked, genuinely puzzled, as they left the last sheltering tree behind and swung off on to the coast road, where a bleak little wind whipped in to send before it the already bending branches of the grey-branched skeletons of trees optimistically planted long ago to take away the arid bareness of this stretch of shore.

'I like looking at houses that are up for sale, and this one is empty and rather interesting,

26

to judge by the picture in the agent's window back in Denbarton.'

'You don't want to go all over an empty house in the dark, in *those* clothes, surely?' he exclaimed, alarmed.

'Well, perhaps not, but would you bring me here tomorrow to look over it, Boyd?' she said, thinking that would be better. It would ensure a further date very quickly and make a successful impact on the watching eyes at the hospital. 'I do so like empty houses.'

Boyd saw danger in that, too, though he couldn't have said why. He shied away from the suggestion, perhaps a little too quickly. 'I'm not free tomorrow, Thora. You know that.'

She bit her lip, angry with herself. There was no need to put him on the defensive like that. Don't push him too hard. Let well done alone.

'No, I forgot that. Sorry, Boyd. Let's just stop and have a peep at it from the gate, shall we?'

Again he capitulated to prevent another date being made, and agreed with her.

The ground had hardened after the last rains. It was rutty, loose stones rattled underfoot. Thora went through the gate, and turned to speak to him, not watching the uneven ground. Her high heel slipped off a rut in the path and she almost went

27

down, falling against him as he went forward to help her.

She had often wondered what he would do in such a situation – would he forget to be wary, and hold her with his arms round her? Or just let her trip over and make a clumsy job of trying to help her up?

His reaction surprised her. His hands shot out and gripped her arms, holding her until she regained her balance, but keeping her at arm's length just the same. It was so neatly and silently done, she couldn't be sure if he thought it was a trick on her part and he had combated it like that, or whether he had simply acted like that by accident. There was no way of telling. His face was expressionless in the moonlight as she broke away from him.

'Are you hurt?' he asked, with a clinical interest that further infuriated her.

She put her foot to the ground. 'No, it's all right, thanks! Sorry, that was stupid of me,' she muttered furiously.

'Yes, well, that's what comes of wanting to look at empty houses in an outfit like that,' he said, with maddening reasonableness.

She looked up after a minute and grinned at him. 'Now I *know* you haven't any womenfolk in your life, or you wouldn't be so reasonable and logical.'

There was just the tiniest pause before he answered, but when he did, he neither refuted that nor accepted it. He merely said mildly, 'It's as well one of us is reasonable and logical.' He put his hands in his pockets and stared disparagingly up at the dark face of the house. 'It's not a very bright idea, surely, to want to look at that shabby old place, and risk ruining those shoes, or turning your ankle.'

'Oh, all right, let's go back!' she said shortly, losing patience with him. It had been a fruitful idea if he had responded to possible ankle turnings, or the romantic looking into empty rooms through the bare glass of the windows, and discussing empty houses in general, perhaps one in particular in the future. But you could only do that with a man who was more than half way willing to whip up some sort of interest. Boyd had mentioned her shoes as though he thought they weren't very sensible; he could have called them 'expensive shoes', or even 'beautiful shoes' but just 'those shoes' was enough to make even her optimism wane.

She let him drive her back to the hospital, where she could give time and thought to where she had gone wrong. She was so sure he was ready for going this stage further. He had even agreed to pick her up at the hairdressers. No, it was from there that he had slipped back to his old elusiveness.

She decided she had moved a little too quickly in her treatment of him. She must go more slowly, use a little intelligence instead of eagerness, she told herself savagely.

She forgot the matter of his lost gloves. Boyd thought of nothing else. He had remembered where he had left them; on the chair in front of Mrs Roberts' desk. He had been wondering how he could approach her to take up that fruitful conversation about Deirdre, and now he had a perfect excuse. He had a pair of lost gloves to collect.

He went to bed early and lay flat on his back with his hands loosely behind his head, watching the patterns of the car headlamps' beams going across his bedroom ceiling, and he tried to work out what made the smile of Mrs Roberts so very special.

He couldn't remember what else her face was like. It was just that warm smile, which invited one to smile back and get to know her. Oh, and her voice. Yes, that was another thing he had noticed. It was warm like her smile, and she spoke rather slowly, not the quick staccato way Thora had. Thora's voice was light weight and like raindrops pattering. Mrs Roberts' voice was like, what? Velvet?

He was half asleep by then. He realized he was very tired. He had been sitting up late by a child's bedside two nights ago; last night they had lost the kidney boy. The blanket of sleep almost claimed him, when a last thought occurred to him. *Mrs* Roberts.

There was a husband around. No, perhaps she was a widow, he corrected himself hopefully, and on that note he fell asleep.

Perhaps for the first time for a very long while, he leapt out of bed with eagerness and told himself it was a wonderful day. He remembered last night and the lost gloves, and wouldn't let himself think that she probably had a husband in that house in Endell Street. After all, he only wanted to talk to her about her sister. She *was* the close relative of a patient, and young Deirdre Arden had interested him very much. The surgeons hadn't done much for her beyond the operation. Let's see what the physicians can do, he decided, and he started to whistle as he brushed his hair.

Professor Barnsley was crossing to the Path Lab. His hair – grey and too long – blew in the wind and looked very untidy. Boyd's hair was usually not very tidy, too, but today he looked unusually neat. The Professor noticed the difference at once. 'Where are you off to?' he asked.

'To pick up my gloves. I lost them yesterday,' Boyd said, looking rather happy about it.

'At this time of the morning? The theatre will be shut!'

'I didn't lose them at the theatre. Before then.'

'Oh.' Professor Barnsley fell into step

beside him. 'Did you have an enjoyable time? Play any good?'

'Not bad. They got their medical data more or less right which is something,' Boyd said, smiling broadly.

Professor Barnsley felt distinctly gloomy. Surely that Fenton woman hadn't managed to charm him so much that he was looking idiotically pleased with everything this chilly morning?

'Have you had your breakfast already?' he asked Boyd.

'No, I forgot my breakfast,' Boyd said, thinking. 'I daresay I could get something in that little shop at the end of the High Street. Well, it'll be a change. There was a very good smell of eggs and bacon and tomatoes there yesterday as I passed.'

'I'll come with you,' the Professor said anxiously.

Boyd looked really put out, his old friend noticed. 'No, old fellow, I'd rather be alone. Got a knotty problem to think over. See you later,' he said vaguely and walked straight on. The Professor stood staring after him in dismay. Even Boyd's back view looked different, tidier, somehow, the professor couldn't help noticing.

Boyd marched down the High Street thinking about Deirdre Arden. Thora had seen her last. Thora, he remembered, didn't seem to make much impression on the women patients. There was a frosty atmosphere. That surprised him. She was a very good doctor, infinitely painstaking with real symptoms, but if she thought the patient was making a lot of her symptoms, Thora got a trifle brusque. Funny, he hadn't really noticed that before now.

But Deirdre Arden, as he remembered, was no hysteric. His thoughts took him marching past the hairdressing salon, still closed and shuttered, and down Endell Street. He walked down the length of the street and up the other side, and he glanced across at the second house as he came back.

It looked like all the others, a square, solid Victorian type villa, with casement windows, a door in the middle of the frontage, a pocket handkerchief lawn with a few bushes, and a wooden gate at each side, one leading to the front door, one to the side entrance. The windows were covered with thick net curtains, shutting out passers by. He wondered what sort of breakfast they were having, and realized he was very hungry.

He shuddered at the thought of the breakfast he would get at the hospital, the sort of breakfast he had been having for so long. Good food badly cooked. Scorched porridge and overdone eggs and bacon. Cold tea, drunk with a newspaper in front of one, or the notes of a case. Talking to one's fellows about the cases. Talking in the same dreary way about the same dreary subjects. That was what came of living in Residents. They talked about how short of money they were, or of how much they deplored leaving wives and families in digs or at home with their families, while they themselves lived in Residents. Boyd could have carried on a specimen conversation at any time. He knew them all. Clutton was fed-up with his brother-in-law always borrowing, and Jewson was always talking about his bank balance being in the red. Vales and Halliday talked cars – the low-slung racing kind – and dreamed of the day when they might just possibly afford one.

He sighed and walked back to the High Street, to the little shop with the window so plastered with advertisements that it was almost impossible to see inside.

Now there was a good smell coming out, of bacon delicately frying. He pushed open the door and the smell was intensified. A fat woman behind the counter at the end greeted him heartily. 'Come along in, sir,' she invited. 'We're open!'

He bought cigarettes, and looked long-ingly in the direction of the frying sounds and smells.

'You've not had breakfast!' she accused him and pointed to a small table against the wall, an iron table with a marble top. It had

34

two old-fashioned bentwood chairs pushed into it. 'Just you sit down there and I'll get you something. I've got tea made. Will that do?'

Do! If her tea was as good as the frying back there, it would more than do, he thought, as he stretched his long legs under the table.

It was an interesting little shop. A skinny girl of about twelve came in for a pint of milk and a tin of pipe tobacco. A boy of eight came in and had difficulty selecting a notebook out of a box of varied sized ones under the counter, and a big girl arrived with a jar to buy something that looked like runny red jam. Two other men came in for breakfast. The fat woman found another chair, and told Boyd he would have to tuck his long legs in and they'd all do nicely, and then she brought the three of them each a plate of bacon, tomatoes, eggs and mushrooms, and a great plate of buttered toast. 'Rough and ready,' she said, and turned to greet another customer. Mrs Roberts.

Chapter Two

Boyd stumbled to his feet, but other people came in the shop and got between them, and anyway, she was too preoccupied to notice him, so he quietly sat down again and watched her. She hadn't got her hair pulled back today. It was hanging loosely on her shoulders. It turned under at the ends, and made her look much younger. She had the sort of figure that looks nice in slacks without being too thin, and her slacks were very trim indeed. She wore a casual sweater with a polo neck and she asked the fat woman anxiously, 'Have you got half a stale loaf left? It's for Kathy! I daren't give her new bread. You know what she's like!'

The fat woman said she'd cut half of her own loaf left from yesterday. 'It's all right, dear, you could have it all if you wanted it,' but Mrs Roberts didn't want it all. Just half. They wrangled pleasantly over meat cubes and boiled sweets, then she turned to go, and saw Boyd. He again stumbled to his feet.

'Hello, Dr Ingram! What are you doing having breakfast here – don't they feed you right at the hospital?' she said, blurting it out in surprise, but so pleasantly that he laughed and the other men sharing the table laughed, and she added, 'It looks good. We didn't have a breakfast like that this morning! I'm not a very good housekeeper.'

He couldn't believe that, and said so. The fat woman joined in. 'Don't take any notice of her, sir,' she said. 'She's a real nice little cook and the way she manages for that family of hers, well!' She shook her head at Mrs Roberts who laughed and hurried out. 'Marchant's have got the book Kathy wanted,' she went to the door to call after the girl. 'If you want to knock at the side door, save you stopping later and then young Kathy could take it to school with her!' The girl's voice sang a reply.

Yes, her voice *sang*, Dr Ingram thought, happiness soaring within him. He got up and paid for his breakfast, and supposed he'd better go back to the hospital, but he really wanted to talk about that girl.

The fat woman said, 'Such a nice girl. Such a shame!' and looked at him for agreement on that point.

'About her sister, you mean? Yes, well, we shall have to see what we can do about that,' he said, nodding.

'Oh, yes, she did call you "doctor",' the fat woman said, on a note of interrogation. 'You'd be at the hospital, then? Oh, if only you *could* make young Deirdre walk again, sir,' she sighed. 'Such a *nice* family! And so tragic.'

Other people were all around him. It was a busy time. He decided to save his questions about Mrs Roberts' family for some other, slacker time. He nodded and went out, conscious that this end of the High Street would see more of him in future. It was like going home. Nice people.

The Professor was waiting for him, still looking puzzled, so he gave himself up to the problem of the boy with the fractured leg. It wasn't a very hard thing to do. It was a most absorbing case. They talked about it on and off during the day. The Professor was isolating a similar bug. When he discovered that the boy's father was a seaman off a tanker from the Middle East, he was quite sure it was the one in which he was interested. But Jason Quinn, one of the consultants who did the round that morning, was quite sure it was bone erosion.

'His pet thing,' Boyd muttered in disgust. 'You'll lose your Bug,' he told his old friend. 'That boy will be whipped off to Alice Mary Holmes Ward, and you won't get a look-in.'

The Professor was very angry and said he would forbid it. Boyd reminded him that Jason Quinn had a cousin on the Board who would back him up in whatever he wanted to do. They gave it up for the day and Boyd went off thinking of that thin little face and the wide dark eyes staring up at him. What was that child thinking about, lying there like that? Across his notes were the words, in red ink: 'Speaks no English.' Speaks no English, but Boyd was quite certain that wasn't to say that the child didn't understand a certain amount.

After lunch that day, the visitors came. Boyd was escaping to the Path Lab again when he saw Mrs Roberts. He had forgotten to ask about his gloves this morning, so he made the excuse of drifting over to her. She was wearing a neat suit of a nondescript brownish-grey. A serviceable colour, he remembered his old nurse used to call it. But it was rather nice. The skirt had pleats all round it, and they bounced in and out as she walked, and the jacket was well enough cut. Her back was ramrod straight, and her hair lifted a little in the jolliest way, he thought, as she walked. She was much younger than he had at first supposed, seeing her sitting so responsibly behind the appointments desk of the hairdressers.

She smiled at him, and now he was waiting for that smile, ready for it, and she didn't disappoint him. 'Hello, Dr Ingram!' she said. 'I'm just going to see my sister.'

'Yes, I know.' That was another thing he wanted to talk to her about. 'I'm going to have a look at her myself.'

She said quickly, and with good reason,

'Deirdre's actually Dr Fenton's patient.'

They exchanged a glance. Both of them knew what that would mean, but he was determined. 'Yes, well,' he said, 'we have been working together on a few cases. I'll go along with her tomorrow and see Deirdre.'

She nodded, and looked rather wistful. Little fragments of memories came back to him. Dr Fenton hadn't liked Deirdre Arden, he recalled. What was it she had said? That the girl's eyes were always on her, and that she couldn't very well accuse her of being impudent, because she didn't say anything, but those eyes could speak volumes. It occurred to Boyd that Thora hadn't realized that Deirdre Arden was Mrs Roberts' sister. The name being different, he supposed.

Suddenly she remembered his gloves. 'Oh, I knew I meant to remember something! I've left your gloves on our hall-stand. I didn't want to leave them at the shop – things get mislaid so easily. Can you wait until the next time I–'

'No, don't worry,' he said quickly. 'I often pass the end of your road. Perhaps I could call and pick them up?'

She agreed, with relief, he thought. It was just another thing she hadn't got to bother to remember to do. But he wanted to call at her home. He wanted to see what it was like, this background of hers. And if the husband happened to be there, he would be able to see what he was like, too. He told himself that it was merely a proprietary interest in the girl, and he wouldn't let himself dwell on it any further.

As RMO, he had to admit patients, and a new one was taken in that afternoon, after the visitors had gone. He went up to the ward with the young woman; one of those unaccountable accidents in the street. She had backed to avoid a lamp falling from some scaffolding, missed her footing, and fallen backwards into the road. The oncoming bicycle had sent her reeling from a glancing blow, and the subsequent fall had done more injury to her back than the bike could have done.

She was put in the bed next to Deirdre. Deirdre was agitating to be allowed to get into a wheelchair and potter about the ward and help the over-worked staff. As she was in under observation, she had to lie still, and she was chafing, every inch of the way.

He went over to her bed. 'It's Mrs Roberts' sister, isn't it?' he smiled.

Deirdre smiled blazingly up at him. Very much like her sister, in that fleeting moment. 'That's right. Only she isn't called that, except in her job,' Deirdre said.

'I see,' he encouraged. 'And what do you do at home that is making you so eager to get about here? Have you got a fairly mobile chair?'

'Yes, I've got a super one. Rachel saved up for it,' she said, without enthusiasm. 'But at home I do almost everything, except get up and down stairs, of course. Someone's got to help Rachel. Besides, it doesn't give me time to think. Only here, there's nothing else to do but think,' she finished bitterly. 'I wish they'd let me go home. They won't be able to do anything!'

'We might,' he said quietly. 'I'm going to have a look at you next time Dr Fenton comes over.'

'That'll be the day! She's seen me. I don't suppose she'll come any more, not this time. I heard her tell Sister I'd have to come back in six months.'

He frowned. 'I'll speak to Sister,' he began, but she broke in, 'No, don't bother. I shouldn't have said that. I shouldn't have been listening. Only Dr Fenton's got the sort of voice that you can hear for miles.'

That was true, he thought ruefully. Thora's voice certainly carried, and he hadn't the nerve to warn her that the patients might hear and worry. He said, 'Still, I'd like to have a look at you, though of course I can't promise anything.'

'I wouldn't mind if they'd let me be getting on with my work!' she exploded.

'Work? What work?'

'Oh, I do things, art and crafts, paint things on bookmarks, soft toys, that sort of thing.

42

Well, there's a lot outstanding and Rachel takes them into the Gift Shop in Astonmore for me, once a month. I won't be ready!'

'I'll see about that, too,' he promised.

'Why should you?' she asked, suddenly suspicious.

'Didn't your sister mention me? We had a few words while she was waiting and I told her I'd have a look at you.'

'Oh, yes. Yes she did. I remember,' she said, with an odd look at him which made him wonder just what her sister had said to her about him.

Thora was waiting for him to go on the promised visit to the empty house that afternoon. Again he had forgotten it. He said, 'Well, all right, but if I do put off what I wanted to do, will you do something for me in return, Thora?' and he smiled at her.

'All right, anything,' she promised recklessly. She tied a bright green chiffon scarf round her hair, against the onslaught of the wind. 'And because you're being so sweet, let's forget about that beastly little house and let's just go for a drive, shall we? And tea somewhere.'

He hardly noticed what she was proposing, he was full of the thought of Deirdre Arden. 'That patient I admitted this morning is in bed beside Deirdre Arden. I spoke to Deirdre. Can't you let her do a few things to keep her occupied, handicrafts?'

43

She frowned. 'Is this what you wanted me to do, Boyd?'

'No, I'll come to that later. Why can't she do things? It's of some importance to her financially, I gather.'

'I know you are RMO but you have never interfered with my patients before, Boyd.'

'I thought we liked looking at some of the interesting ones together. Was I wrong?' he murmured.

'Not at all. I thought so, too,' she agreed heartily.

'Well, then?'

'Well, what, Boyd? I would hardly call Deirdre Arden an interesting one. If you want to know, she's an hysteric. She could walk if she wanted to, but that sister of hers is pushing all the time so we go through the farce of having the girl in under observation. Nothing comes of it because she won't try.'

'Oh, you knew who her sister was, then?'

'Boyd, you don't listen to me. I told you who the sister was. The whole family are a lot of pests. Let's not encourage them.'

'You know the family?' He was surprised.

'Who doesn't?' Thora retorted. 'They practically live in the hospital, though heaven knows how they come to have so many sick relatives and friends. But there, if you look hard enough, every hospital has at least one family like that. Gracious, how did we get on to the subject of Mrs Roberts?'

He was quick to notice her tone. 'Don't you like her, Thora?'

'Do you?' she was quick to fling back at him.

'I hardly know her, do I, but you appear to know her and her family very well, and I always like to hear your assessment of people.'

She was mollified by his tone, and considered the question. 'Yes, well, they've had their share of bad luck I suppose. But no, I can't say I like Mrs Roberts. Not honestly, that is, and you know I'm honest, Boyd, don't you?'

He said he did but he didn't sound very pleased. It was Thora who broke the silence again. 'Let's not make a "thing" of that family, Boyd. If you want to go and have a look at that girl, then let's arrange the thing by all means. You'll see I'm right. She could help herself but won't.'

He didn't mind what happened now. He had got her agreement to share the patient with him, and he had just remembered that he was to go to the house in Endell Street to pick up his gloves. He was absurdly thrilled about it, and told himself pretty sharply that he might well run straight into the husband and that would be the end of that. End of what, he asked himself sharply? What did he expect from this?

He missed a lot of what Thora was saying,

in his anxiety to search his motives. He wanted, he discovered, just to know Mrs Roberts more. He wanted to help her, if he could, but most of all, he wanted to enjoy the warmth of her personality. She was one of those people it is just a delight to be *with*.

Thora seemed satisfied, too. She was a very attractive person when she was pleased. She told him about her Uncle Ewart, who had an interest in a rather plushy clinic in London and wanted someone go-ahead to run it. It seemed to her that Boyd had expressed interest all the time she was talking. She would have been very put out if she had realized he had been thinking about her new hairdresser's receptionist. Boyd smiled happily, if vaguely, in Thora's direction, in the way he did when most of his attention was on the driving, so she received the impression that he, too, shared her desire to get out of Denbarton and taste London at its best.

'I thought you'd be interested,' she said, in a pleased voice. 'He isn't hard up, you know. I don't know if I ever told you but he owns the Langdale Institute.'

Boyd brought himself up sharply. What had Thora been talking about? He said, 'You never told me that before,' which sounded intelligent.

Thora was a little surprised, but pleased. So money and position *did* weigh with Boyd, after all. 'I thought I had,' she said easily. 'Of course, a lot of the money belonged to my aunt, but it's all in the family. He's got young Max Trent under his wing, although that didn't please his father, who owns a surgical instrument factory and wanted Max to train to step into his shoes when he retires.'

Now Boyd was alarmed. He had missed the thread altogether. 'Max Trent – did you say?' he felt carefully along the verbal path they had come without his noticing.

'Oh, Boyd, my cousin Max. Lucille's brother! You remember I told you about Lucille Stevens who crashed her husband's car while he was in the Middle East? He was livid. All he could think of was the car bill and the damage – not a word about poor Lucille suffering from delayed shock for positively *days*.'

'When was this?' he asked idly. He didn't know this Lucille who didn't sound a very responsible driver, and he was rather surprised that Thora, who was so punctilious about everything, should take this person's part so savagely.

Thora looked taken aback at his question, and didn't answer for the moment. Then she said, 'Oh, it was a year ago, or thereabouts,' and she suddenly dropped the subject.

Thora, he thought, at random, wasn't a very comfortable person to be with nowadays, yet she had seemed so at first. He thought about the time when she had taken him up, a lonely new boy at the hospital in a town that was rather hybrid; a town that had long since ceased to be small, yet had become enlarged in a straggling way. Not as big as Oddenport, but big enough to make a stranger feel lonely, and hopelessly shy. He had avoided the social club, and the hospital's rather large sports club. He had never fancied himself clowning about in the quarterly theatrical production. Performing for the benefit of the patients had never been his line. He had made a quick and satisfying friendship with the Professor, but that wasn't so astonishing, since he had been corresponding with the Professor long before he had come to Denbarton. The Professor's books had intrigued him enough to want to make contact, if only through correspondence, with the person who had written them.

And then he had met Thora through his work; a plain looking, no nonsense type of woman doctor who had seemed dedicated. Well, that was the first impression he had got. Later, over the weeks, he came to see that she was rather more worldly than she had at first permitted him to realize. He fancied she was more interested in social climbing in London through a smart appointment, than in taking advantage of the real work on the wards here in Denbarton.

But Thora had recovered herself now, and

made the rest of the drive so pleasant, that by the time they went into the secluded corner of the restaurant to enjoy a quiet cup of tea, his fears were lulled again. He was not, by temperament, a man who liked to look for trouble. He just wanted peace, and time and good companionship to enjoy his work.

As soon as they got back to Denbarton, the thought of those gloves came into his mind again, and as soon as he could decently get away from Thora, he walked round to the house in Endell Street.

Today the front door stood open. A supercilious cat sat there, and the hall – gleaming with fresh white paint, on walls and woodwork, the floor a sea of warm red carpet whose colour was echoed in a bowl of red roses on a table in front of a long mirror – surprised him. A young man walked very slowly round the house, apparently as supercilious as the cat in the open doorway.

And then the young man stopped, in an attitude of listening. 'Is someone there?' he asked sharply.

His sightless eyes looked straight ahead of him, not to where Boyd stood. Boyd said quietly, 'Don't be alarmed. I'm a doctor from the hospital. Mrs Roberts said I could call and pick up the gloves I left in the place where she works.'

The young man's face cleared. 'Oh. Oh,

yes, I remember – you must be Dr Ingram. Am I right? Then you'd better come in.'

Boyd strolled towards him and took his elbow. The young man gently inched away. 'No, don't touch me, please. Point of honour that I walk round the house at least once a day without any help at all, and that I don't trip over that damned cat or its kittens.'

'You should use a white stick,' Boyd said gently.

'No!' the young man said sharply. 'No, that makes it all seem so final, and me just a helpless wreck. No, other people have learned to get around without advertising the fact that they can't see, and so will I.'

Boyd was conscious of sharp disappointment. Was this the husband? Then in that case there would be no friendship between himself and Rachel. This fellow didn't deserve that.

If he himself were blind, and as gallant as this chap, he wouldn't want to feel that his wife had men friends. He said, 'Well, if you're sure you can manage–'

'I've got to,' the young man said grimly. 'Rachel's probably watching me at this very minute, from where she works.'

Boyd Ingram looked up the road to his left. Yes, the hairdressers' window could be seen, though he couldn't see the reception desk. He said, with a sigh, 'Yes, well, perhaps *you* can tell me where your wife left my gloves, Mr Roberts.'

The young man turned his face round to Boyd's, frowning a little. 'Rachel's not my wife, she's my cousin,' he said. 'I thought you knew that, Dr Ingram. I'm Neil Upcroft.'

Again Boyd felt a rush of feeling, this time of relief. He hadn't wanted Rachel to be tied to such a burden, though he was quite sure she wouldn't complain herself.

'I think,' Neil said, 'if you've the time, you might as well come in. Rachel herself will be home soon. She'll want to talk to you, I expect. About Deirdre.'

'Oh, yes, her sister,' Boyd said, and followed him into the house.

He glanced round him as they went through to the back. There was a pretty sitting-room in grey and old rose, all freshly painted, pristine neat, and a starkly simple dining-room. Another door stood open on a small box of a room that was not neat by any standards. It contained a desk and a table, three chairs, and such an overflow of papers that it made the head reel; whose study was this? Rachel's?

The young man led him to the kitchen. A big room running right across the back of the house. This was painted pale yellow and green, a room made to catch the sunshine.

'I say, this is a jolly nice room,' Dr Ingram said.

'Is it? I don't know. I've never seen it. The

girls were talking about green and yellow when they did it. Describe it to me, sir, if you will, while I make you some tea. Do say you'd like some – I'm terrific at making it!'

Yes, it was easy to see he was a blood relation of Rachel. He had the same engaging manner, and those eyes must have been the same intense blue, dancing with fun, when they had any sight in them. Boyd felt his usual wave of anger wash over him at the waste, the shocking waste, in cases like these.

Neil went confidently to where the electric kettle was and filled it. 'The girls are pretty dab at painting, you know. Deirdre does as far as she can reach, and Rachel climbs up and does the rest. They've got a passion for keeping the house well painted, in case they ever have to sell it, you know. It belongs to us. It was left us by Rachel's parents.'

'I see. Well, they've done an astonishingly good job. I would never have known it wasn't a professional job. It's yellow, as you say, but the number of shelves and cupboards – they surely didn't – no, of course not!'

'A neighbour's son helped them.' He went a little pink as he said it. Boyd wondered what that meant. He went on describing the room while he watched Neil.

'It's a very cheerful room indeed,' he said, in a pleased way. 'I like the idea of sliding doors to the cupboards. Very sensible. I suppose – er – you're used to cats and kittens about the place.'

'I do fall over them, if that's what you mean,' Neil said coolly, 'but I'd rather that than be without them. They're company. We also have a dog, but he seems to have got out. It's bedlam sometimes, the dog chasing the cats. But it amuses the girls. We have to keep Deirdre amused, you know. She has a passion for keeping on the go. So do I, really. Not quite the same, but in my fashion I keep on the move.'

'Can nothing be done?' Boyd said, feeling useless. Usually people just sat pathetically waiting for someone to suggest a miracle, or else they were bitterly dependent, making you feel it was your fault. This young man was neither. He had reduced his inability to see, to a dignified slightly slow but confident set of movements, more like an important personage not deigning to hurry, rather than a blind man fumbling his way through life.

'Nothing,' Neil said firmly. 'Dear Dr Fenton procured a top eye specialist to prove that nothing could be done.'

Boyd was startled. 'She did? You were her patient, then?'

'No, I was not. I was at Oddenport General and she had me transferred to Denbarton.'

'Why?' Boyd was very anxious to know why such a thing should be done. 'I mean,

53

are you friends of hers – this family I mean? I am aware that she knows you all because of Deirdre, and because of ... Mrs Roberts.'

'I will tell you why. Because she is a do-gooder, and because she was very anxious to prove that if anything could be done, she was the one to do it.'

A stony silence fell on the room. Boyd closed his lips in a tight line. Neil said, 'That was ill-behaved of me, sir, because I believe Dr Fenton is a friend of yours. I had no right to say that, even though I believe it. Please forgive me.'

Boyd got up. 'There's nothing to forgive, though I wish you hadn't said it. What puzzles me is why Dr Fenton should have gone to so much trouble. I mean, she must have known one of you rather well. Mrs Roberts, perhaps.'

Neil appeared to have lost interest. He was concentrating on making the tea. 'Perhaps,' he agreed, and put out a hand unerringly to the fridge door and got the milk out.

'Would you like to tell me what happened – how the accident happened, I mean? Don't worry, if you feel you can't talk about it. I can always ask Dr Fenton.'

'Yes, you'd better do that, sir,' Neil said, and now there was no need for him to feign concentration. He had made the tea with precision and tidiness, set a tray, poured out, and brought the tray to the table, undeterred by the fact that three kittens had run up his person and were clinging to him like burrs.

'I'll take those off you,' Boyd offered, but Neil said, 'I wish you wouldn't. It's a sort of afternoon marathon race, to see who can reach my shoulder first. I enjoy it as much as they do.' So Boyd took his tea and sat down and began to ask about Deirdre. 'What did she do by way of a living before the accident?'

'She was a student nurse at Oddenport General Hospital,' Neil said. 'She hadn't been there long – a matter of weeks. She never speaks of it now, and neither does anyone else. It's over.'

Boyd was shocked. 'And you yourself – what was your profession?'

'Me? Oh, I'm lucky. Practically the same as it is now. Journalism, only of course it's freelance. It has to be. I can no longer rush out and report a fire, because such a report stating: "I could feel the heat and hear the crackling of the fire and they tell me it took place at" – would shock my dear old editor, who isn't really progressive. Still, it might be startling, at that, don't you think, sir. I never thought of that before.'

He wasn't being bitter, just dryly amused. Boyd was silent, watching him, drinking his tea. Neil went on, 'I expect you want to know how I manage to keep on writing since I can't see the things I do write about. Well, poor old Rachel, good old Faithful, reads the newspapers to me, and cuts out the articles and bits I tell her to, and makes the files up for me, and when she has the time she goes to the Public Library and looks up the things I ask for, and I write articles hinged on current news items. I will not be a financial drag on this family!' and that last sentence was the very first time he had sounded in any way angry or bitter.

'And you type the things yourself?' Boyd hazarded. 'Why look surprised? I've no doubt you've taught yourself to manage a good many things for yourself. I applaud your tenacity, but I wish you would let me try to find out–'

'*No;* do not, please, sir. Dr Fenton has said I am doomed to be like this forever. Do let's leave well alone. I don't distrust her,' but his tone belied his words.

And then they heard footsteps coming up the path. Neil said, 'Ah, here's Kathy coming home from school. Another relative.'

Kathy bounced in, throwing things as she came. Boyd heard her satchel being dumped on the floor, and saw a boater whiz past the open door, not quite getting a bull's eye on the hatstand. Neil called, with weary patience, 'Pick them all up and stow them away, please.'

Kathy appeared, sullen, and picked up the

56

things. Then, realizing a stranger was in the kitchen, she bounced back and stared at him, her eyebrows raising, as Boyd got up. 'Oh, who is this dear man?' she murmured. 'He's a honey. How did *you* manage to find him, dear Neil?'

'Shut up, Kathy,' Neil said, with that weary big-brother air. 'This is Dr Ingram from the hospital. The owner of the gloves Rachel brought home from the shop.'

Kathy wasn't a bit like Rachel. Kathy was a big girl, with long blonde hair that curled (or was curled) tightly on the ends, in a rather provocative way. She had provocative eyes and lips, a handful altogether, Boyd thought, and although she was only about fifteen, she was big-made and would be handsome on maturity.

Boyd said hello to her, in a friendly way. 'Kathy Arden?' he asked, to make sure he got the name right.

That surprised her. 'No, of course not. Kathy Roberts,' she said. So Boyd concluded that this must be the young sister of Rachel's husband. He said a few kind things to the girl, but she merely stood and stared at him and at Neil, as if trying to assess what they had been talking about.

Neil said at last, 'If you're still there, Kathy, don't you think you'd better go? Get washed for tea or something, get your homework done. You *do* waste time.'

'Yes, and I must go,' Boyd said. Rachel would soon be home and she wouldn't want a visitor here, probably with the husband coming home for a meal which she would have to cook. He said, 'I expect Mrs Roberts and her husband will both be glad to see the back of an uninvited visitor.'

Kathy looked sharply at him. Neil appeared to be going to say something but Kathy got in first. 'No, Rachel won't mind a visitor. Deirdre's in hospital, and there's no husband.'

Boyd said he'd go just the same and he struggled to keep the pleasure out of his voice, because although the thought of Rachel being a widow might be very acceptable to him, it did mean, after all, that this girl's big brother was dead. No wonder the poor kid was insecure, provocative, a little truculent, and hating being held down by a young man like Neil, who wasn't even related to her.

'Go and have a shot at that homework, Kathy,' he said kindly. 'If you can't do it, perhaps next time I'm this way I'll try and help you.'

Kathy walked to the door with him. 'Why will you do that?' she asked curiously. 'I mean, are you interested in our Deirdre?'

Chapter Three

The Professor knew something of the accident. He seemed curiously reluctant to talk about it.

'It was just before you came, you know,' he said, looking curiously at Boyd. 'Why don't you ask Mrs Roberts to tell you about it?'

'Well, why would I do that, and risk upsetting her, if you can tell me just as easily?' Boyd asked, squinting through the microscope at the Professor's latest effort.

'You have a point,' he remarked dryly. 'Well, the young man who was blinded, appeared to have been a pedestrian at the time, and his cousin, who seems to have aroused your sudden interest was in someone's car and thrown out, as an oncoming car collided head on. But in being thrown out she was run over by another car that swerved to avoid the one she was in. Unfortunate, altogether.'

'Oh, no!' Boyd murmured, shocked. As RMO he saw so many of these victims coming into Casualty. It was he who admitted them. He could see the accident in his mind's eye. 'The driver of the car that Deirdre was with – what happened to him?'

Now he had got the idea fixed in his mind that it was Mrs Roberts' husband and that that was the way he died.

'Now, really, old fellow, I don't think I should tell you that, because you happen to be interested in someone who belonged to him. So let's let it go, shall we?' the Professor said. So to Boyd, that was confirmation.

He wanted to ask about the other car, but Professor Barnsley clearly didn't want to discuss it. He said, 'Did you get your gloves?'

'Yes. No! Oh, dash, I've just remembered – I left them there after all.' On the hall table, when Kathy walked him to the door and asked if he were interested in Deirdre…

The Professor chuckled. 'Never mind, a good excuse to go back for them again.'

Boyd went on to the wards feeling happy for the first time for ages. He had several very interesting cases that absorbed him. There was the boy with the fractured leg, and the 'bug' the Professor had discovered. There was the girl who was being steadily fed less, on a special diet, to reduce her weight, but who grew heavier every day. There were two men with a disease from the Middle East that was causing grave anxiety on the ward, but stimulated the interest of Boyd and the Professor so that they forgot the time and talked for hours in the Path Lab. Thora stifled her exasperation and gave herself a time limit before she said anything. But when Boyd left the hospital he vanished.

She didn't notice it at first. When she did, she allowed a week to pass and asked him where he had been. He looked vague, and a little surprised. Nettled, she said, 'I suppose you've been drooling over the child that Roberts woman brought in! Well, he's being taken care of. You don't need to worry. They are going to transfer him to Oddenport General.'

Too late she saw that she had said the wrong thing. 'What child did Mrs Roberts bring in?' he asked, very quietly.

'Oh, just a neighbour's child,' she said carelessly.

'When, Thora? And why didn't I know about it?'

'Because you were off duty, messing about in that horrible corner of the Path Lab with your friend Professor Barnsley, and some-one else was doing your duty and acted with a bit of sense,' she snapped. 'Boyd, where do you vanish to when you go off duty? I've been wanting to speak to you about something private and personal.'

He didn't say where he had been. He just thought about Mrs Roberts bringing in a neighbour's child. 'I went to see some old friends of mine,' he said without really thinking about it.

'But I didn't know you *had* any old friends in this district,' she protested.

'Oh, yes, one or two,' he said, without enlightening her. 'Look, my dear, I'd love to hear all about this child that your Mrs Roberts brought in but there's something I have to do. I'll talk to you later.'

'I'm off duty now,' she said eagerly. 'I'll come with you.'

'I don't think that would answer, my dear,' he said, smiling faintly, and was surprised to see Thora blush with embarrassment. He realized he had snubbed her. 'Oh, Thora, I didn't mean to be so brusque. I've just thought of something I forgot to go over with the Professor, that's all. You know you'd hate to come with me to that particular place.'

'Oh, is that all? How long will you be?' she asked him.

'Don't wait for me, my dear. Tell me about this thing some other time when my mind is free to give my full attention to it,' he begged.

She had to let him go. She watched him out of sight, a tall, rangy figure, with a slightly loping walk when he was deep in thought. He was back in his shabby clothes; once good tweeds, but now sadly needing to be thrown out. He looked so comfortable in them that she could have shaken him. Besides, there were many windows from which eyes were probably watching the RMO escaping from Dr Fenton, she thought savagely, well aware that the nursing staff would see the significance and be amused, even if the patients didn't.

She watched him vanish in the distance into the door of the Path Lab and only then was she satisfied. But she didn't check how long he stayed there.

Boyd found his old friend abstractedly making notes by his microscope. 'I forgot to ask you,' he said suddenly, not looking up at Boyd. 'You left a letter here. Was it important? I'm afraid I've scribbled notes all over it, and I don't want to let it go now. Do you want it?'

'Well, that's what I came back for,' Boyd said worriedly. 'I thought I might have dropped it here. Just let me have the letter and you can keep the envelope.'

'I used the letter too. Sorry, but I had a pressing need for something to write on and I couldn't find my pad.'

'Oh, well,' Boyd shrugged, 'just let me make a note of the times and dates mentioned. It's from a school.'

'I know. I'm afraid I absently read it. I looked to see if it was a bill I ought to pay.'

'Oh, well, so now you know that I have to go and meet a child from school. The school don't want her there any more.'

The Professor looked up then. His eyes

were tired, red-rimmed. He took off his glasses and thoughtfully wiped them. 'Oh, well,' he said at last, 'you and I deal with all sorts and kinds of children. This is only one extra kind. Not yours, I suppose?'

'Not mine,' Boyd said between his teeth. 'But I'm responsible for her.' And as the Professor looked faintly surprised, he did what he rarely liked doing and offered some sort of explanation. 'She's my sister's– She's widowed and can't have the child. Asked me to. It's a long story.'

The Professor nodded, satisfied. 'I didn't really think the child would be yours. Burdens, from families, are the very devil. Can't refuse to shoulder 'em, of course. Can't keep her in Residents, either.'

'No,' Boyd agreed feelingly, and wondered what Thora would have said if she had been the one he had given this confidence to and not the Professor.

He was helpful. 'My sister might take her for a few days,' he offered, a little doubtfully. 'But I warn you, Harriet's a mite eccentric. Your girl might finish up that way.'

Boyd's worried face creased into a smile. 'What, after a few days? Much more likely that your sister would finish up going round the bend!'

They both laughed gently, then Boyd took the Professor up on his offer. 'A few days, I'd be grateful, until I can find somewhere permanent to fix her up.'

'A new school?' the Professor asked, consideringly.

'Hardly,' Boyd said, thinking, doing mental arithmetic. 'It's the end of term, as good as, isn't it? I never know. I'll make a rotten guardian.'

'To judge by the noise in the street outside, it will be the end of term for the local schools,' the Professor sighed.

They arranged times and other domestic details, then Boyd went, with a lift of the heart, to the place where he usually escaped to, these last few blessed days; a week, come to think of it, a precious week that he had kept to himself, just for his bits of free time – the house in Endell Street. Sometimes it was to sit and talk with Neil, sometimes to sit with Deirdre, not saying much but watching her clever fingers shape weird but delightful animals out of bits of material and dobs of cotton wool. She had been released from the hospital and got about in her chair just as before, neither complaining nor betraying any hopes or fears for the future. She seemed to have been able to erect a wall around her that even he couldn't pierce.

Today he found young Kathy on her own.

She had been crying. She had changed out of her school uniform and was wearing the queer assortment of clothes favoured by the young. Her skirt was to her ankles and looked to Boyd's astonished eyes as if it were an old dress worn by someone's grandmother. There was a long woollen waistcoat made of coloured medallions sewn together. It had no sleeves and it had been washed too much. Her hair, loose and straight, hadn't been washed enough, and she wore half a dozen assorted gilt necklaces and some jangly bracelets. Her feet were bare and she didn't look as if she could possibly belong to the immaculate Rachel.

She glared at Boyd. 'Nobody's in but me,' she began.

'No-one? Not even Deirdre?'

Kathy shrugged. 'She took herself off in her chair. Thought she'd like to prove something.'

'Shouldn't you have gone with her?'

She looked pityingly at him. 'No, I don't play gooseberry to anyone.'

'What is that supposed to mean?'

'That Hugh Carey came. From the Gift Shop in Astonmore.'

'Oh. Well, if he came, why does Rachel have to spare a day of her precious time, going into Astonmore with the things Deirdre makes?'

'Search me. He's never done it before.'

'Oh. Well, does your sister know? Won't she be worried?'

'*Dear* Dr Ingram, we're an independent lot in this family. We like to manage things

66

for ourselves. Deirdre thought she'd like to wheel herself out today so who stopped her? And I saw this snazzy car stop and Hugh Carey get out, then he locked it and walked by Deirdre's chair, talking to her, but he wasn't fool enough to offer to push it. She'd hate that.'

He smiled faintly. 'Any use asking where Neil is?'

'Gone to the Post Office. Can't trust anyone else to post his precious works of art he writes.'

Boyd stopped smiling. 'I don't think you should talk like that, Kathy. Any man who has to support a family (or help to) by being a freelance writer, lives on the edge of a precipice, I should think.'

'What do you know about it?' she said rudely.

'Me? Oh, I know quite a bit about everything. The patients tell me. I've had freclance journalists confide to me that they liked to post their own work. It's natural. I've also had young people your age confide in me, and the things they fear are not always easy for other people to understand.'

His inviting look was lost on her. 'Look, I said we were an independent lot, and that goes for me, too. All right, I know I look a fright. I've been bawling. But I'll get out of this mess.'

'Can you?' Boyd asked, looking at her

rather critically. 'Is it a bad mess? Sometimes even adults need a bit of help.'

She shrugged again. 'Oh, you want to know what it's about. Well, I might as well tell you. If I don't, Neil will love to. He gave me a ticking off before he went, for good measure. I hate him.'

'How it comes back to me, the times I said that about people who ticked me off and I couldn't hit back,' Boyd said, with a wry smile. 'I don't suppose you really do hate him.'

Kathy glared. 'Nobody understands people of my age. Just because everyone has to go to school, they think it suits everyone! What do I want to learn all that old stuff for – peculiar maths that nobody can work out, but the answers are there anyway – cutting rabbits and frogs up – ugh! Learning daft languages. Who wants to speak them, anyway? I'm wasting time and energy on all that stuff when all I want is–' She broke off and bit her lip.

'What do you want, I wonder?' Boyd mused, looking round the room. It was the immaculate sitting-room. He had noticed that sheet music had been slung around everywhere. He had wondered how it looked different today. 'Oh, yes, I see,' he said. 'Well, it might be a good thing to pick all this up before Rachel gets home.'

'I don't care,' Kathy stormed. 'She sides

with Neil. She says I ought to do my home-work.'

Boyd picked up a piece of Schubert. 'You play this? I wonder if you're really any good at it?' he asked sadly. 'So many people–'

She didn't let him finish. She snatched it from him and put it up on the piano rack and began to play.

She had a gift, he had to admit. She abandoned Schubert after a few bars, and slipped into other, rather more emotional pieces. The more violent of Chopin, bits of Tchaikovsky and Prokofiev; nothing tender or delicate, because she couldn't bang her emotions out on the piano with those. She made the piano rock.

Presently she finished and looked at him, challengingly. 'Well, you certainly *have* something,' he allowed. 'Push over and let's have one half of the stool,' and sat down and played a few delicate bars of Debussy, a bit of Coleridge Taylor, slipping in and out of pieces he had known and loved, but all delicate and beautiful. Nothing crashing and dramatic about his choice of piano music.

'It may not be your kind of music, but if you have hopes of a musical career, you have to learn all sorts, and to someone as mercurial as you, it takes quite a bit of discipline – yes, discipline – to play this sort of thing as it should be. What is it you want to do with your music? No, don't go getting all excited, because *I* don't yet know if you'd ever stay the course, or be able to do what you wanted.'

'Oh, I would, I would, *dear* Dr Ingram, I would! Some of my friends are dotty on horses and some on painting but music's my *Thing*. Nothing else matters.'

'Then that *is* dotty,' he allowed. 'You must get yourself educated, as well as learning about music.'

'But, why, *why?* It's such a waste of *time!*' she wailed.

'How do *you* know? How *can* you know what's a waste of time, when you've only had fifteen years, anyway?' he asked sternly. 'No, no, listen, if I undertake to discuss this with Neil and Rachel, you must leave it to me to do it in my own way, and you must guarantee, on your part, to get on with your ordinary school work and do it well. And don't ask me what *I* know about it, anyway. There's a girl rising up to your age that I am responsible for, and believe me, she's taught me quite a few things about what you young people want.'

Kathy was at once interested. She tucked her unruly hair behind one ear and demanded to know how old this girl was and what her name was.

'She's rising thirteen, her name is Felicity and she has just been expelled from school.

70

Well, that is, I have been asked to remove her from school, which is almost the same thing.'

'What did she do? Something wicked?'

He studied Kathy's face, now alive with interest and that disturbing excitement. 'She was unhappy, insecure,' he said bluntly. 'Her father is dead, and her mother is an actress, a film actress...'

'But how thrilling!'

'...always going away on location,' he continued, with no great liking in his voice. 'Here's the desert, there the Alps, or Arizona, whatever job she happens to have picked up. No, she's not the star.'

'Oh,' Kathy said flatly, and tried to think about it.

'So you see, I shall have to try and be father as well as mother, because although you girls don't admit to it, it's rather nice to have someone to pour your troubles out on to, isn't it, and to tuck you into bed at night? I know at fifteen I would have scorned to admit it, but it was rather pleasant to have my mother's head pop round the door, and to hear her say, "All right, Boyd? Goodnight then, and God Bless." Odd, that I should remember that at this moment,' he said half to himself, as he stared at a picture of Rachel on the mantelpiece. She would be good at saying goodnight, he felt quite sure.

'Aren't you married, then?' Kathy asked,

in her blunt brash way.

'I am not married,' he allowed.

He got up suddenly. 'I've been in this house on quite a few occasions and it seemed a peaceful place. What's it going to be like now you're at home for the holidays, Kathy?'

She grinned. 'Hell,' she said briefly. 'Oh, well,' she said, shrugging her shoulders, 'I like to make a noise, just to show I'm around. Quiet places make me feel uneasy. But Neil's sitting wrapped in thought doing his beastly work and it's still a bit uncanny because his eyes don't see, yet he seems to know what's going on all the time. Then there's Rachel.'

'Yes?' Boyd breathed, and waited.

'Oh, well, Rachel is all motherly and jolly and makes us eat and sees our clothes are aired, and she also tries to see that we're all *mentally* comfortable only it won't work because Neil likes to think of himself as head of the family because he's older than she is...'

'Is he in love with her?' Boyd asked sharply.

'Good heavens, no. He's dotty about Hazel next door. You remember he told you about a neighbour who put the shelves up? That's Hazel's big brother. He only does it because of Hazel and our Neil. Only if you want to know, Hazel's getting a bit fed-up with being in love with someone like Neil who just sits there all silent, listening. She's a bit, well, Go-Go-Go- if you see what I mean.'

'I think I do, Kathy. Is she a piano maniac too?'

'I'm not a piano maniac!' Kathy said hotly, then grinned as he turned to show his face, with that rueful, teasing, half-smile on it. 'Oh, you're getting at me again. No, Hazel's a nut about dancing. Neil used to dance, only, well, like he is – *you* know. Goodness, what's it *like* to be blind?' she burst out suddenly.

'Try tying a black cloth over your head, and getting about, then you'd find out, Kathy,' Boyd said gently, thinking she might be a little more patient with Neil if she did. 'You have to *listen* and *smell* and *touch* and *think*. *Concentrate* would be a better word. And however much you manage to get about without the degrading sense of having to be *taken*, I imagine one would still feel hopelessly out of everything. You can't catch a person's eye to share a joke any more. You have to rely on your senses to know if you're being cheated. It's a dark lonely world, Kathy.'

'I say, you do go into things, don't you?' Kathy said, awestruck. 'I read a book about a king who was worse than blind. He was deaf too. He went mad in the end. I would, too, I think. It was one of the Georges, the third, I think.' She widened her eyes and quickly tucked her curtain of hair back to look up at Boyd. 'I say, I wonder if Neil gets tetchy because he's scared of going deaf too? I say, how awful! No wonder Hazel–' and she clapped her hand to her mouth as she realized where her thoughts were leading her. Undoubtedly the pretty, dance-mad worldly Hazel from next door had thought of such things, more in the light of having to nurse an incapacitated husband. But she would have looked ahead and seen such a possibility.

Kathy jumped up. 'Goodness, it doesn't bear thinking about!' She looked in the glass at herself. 'I look a mess! Why didn't you tell me? What are you going to do with Felicity who's been expelled? I say, are you going to do anything about me, and my music? I'd love your forever if you did. I'd do anything, anything you asked!'

'Kathy, Kathy, for goodness' sake don't say such things! Whether you mean them or not, it doesn't matter! I know I'm not the sort of person you have to fear, but that doesn't mean to say you can trust everyone like that! Hasn't Rachel taught you better?'

She wrinkled up her nose at him in a way that stopped her being a big, sullen girl, and made brief enchantment rest in her eyes. 'You should talk! You've been alone in the house with me all this time and you're lecturing me! Oh, here comes Rachel now, to spoil our tête-à-tête.'

Furious at being caught like that, he turned with relief to the front door. Rachel came in with a bounce. Surprise lit her face, and pleasure, but she was worried, too.

'Oh, Dr Ingram, you here?' Fear shot through her. 'Is something wrong? Deirdre? Neil? *Kathy?*'

'No, they're all right – at least so far as I know the other two are all right. Kathy tells me Neil took his letters to post, and a man from the Gift Shop arrived in his car and walked along by Deirdre's chair.'

'Oh, Hugh Carey,' Rachel said, in relief. 'Yes, he's a nice man. And *Kathy?*'

Kathy came cheekily from behind Boyd. 'He's been lecturing me about the way I play–'

'She shook the piano on its feet in her desire to display her skill for my benefit,' he murmured, his eyebrows raised, as he took Rachel's parcels from her.

'Oh, that.' Rachel frowned. 'I hope you haven't been encouraging her to think she'll make a concert pianist.'

'He's got a girl of thirteen called Felicity whose been expelled from school,' Kathy blurted out. She did tend to blurt, for effect, Boyd decided. She wasn't quite as brash as that.

75

Rachel looked bewildered, then said, 'Yes, well, I'll put the kettle on for some tea, while I gather up Deirdre's things to take to the shop. Oh, I wonder if Hugh Carey is still around? He could take them for us.' She turned to Boyd. 'How long have you been here, Dr Ingram, to give me a guide where to find them.'

'About fifteen, twenty minutes, I suppose,' he said thinking. 'But I don't know when Deirdre went out,' and he turned to Kathy.

She pulled a face. 'Most of that time went on a lecture and a piano lesson,' she complained, 'and yes, I suppose the other two must have just gone when my male guest arrived,' she grinned at Boyd. 'Because I was still bawling after the ticking off Neil gave me. About making a row when he wants to type,' she explained as Rachel stopped to look at her.

Neil came in then. There was a brief exchange of light voices in conversation outside the front door. Rachel said, 'Oh, that will be Deirdre.' She looked out of the window. 'She's alone. Oh, bother – if we'd caught Hugh Carey that would have saved me a journey. Never mind. Wonder what he wanted?' Brief anxiety filled her face again as she opened the door for Neil and Deirdre. She was afraid that Hugh Carey wouldn't want any more of Deirdre's hand-sewn gifts, Boyd thought.

Deirdre looked cool and calm as always. 'Hello, you're home early, Rachel,' she said. 'Guess who walked with me this afternoon?'

'I told them, I told them,' Kathy shouted, tearing up the stairs. Neil winced, and Deirdre looked briefly displeased.

'Oh, well, you know it was Hugh, then.'

'Yes. Pity he couldn't have taken the things back with him, dear,' Rachel said quietly. They had all walked with her to the kitchen. Boyd hung around because he wanted to speak to her about young Kathy, and because she was worried and he had a need to know why. He wouldn't let himself look too deeply into why he should concern himself with the anxieties of this family. He just couldn't tear himself away.

Rachel put, with quick neat movements, cups, saucers, plates on the table, and Neil went to the dresser and got out knives and tea-spoons, and the jam-pot and butter, the bread and bread board. He had to be doing something all the time. Deirdre said, 'I thought of that, Rachel, and I asked him but he's going on to Birmingham. It wouldn't have been any good. He's away for two days and they want them in the shop today.'

'Then it's the bus. I don't think I'll stop for tea,' Rachel said.

'Yes, have your tea,' Boyd insisted. 'I'll be glad to drive you to Astonmore and anywhere else you want to go. It's nice sometimes to get out of the hospital,' he added, for the benefit of the other two who looked surprised.

He wasn't going to relinquish this chance of being with Rachel now. He had some tea with them and helped load the things on to the back seat, and he didn't really feel safe until they had left Endell Street and the town behind them.

Then he eased out. He looked at Rachel, sitting composedly beside him. She had on the muted suit again but a lemon blouse that alleviated the dull colour of the skirt and jacket. Neat and very nice.

She smiled at him. 'What made you come to our house today?' she asked quietly.

'Oh, well, you can't blame me, can you? It's so comfortable and interesting. I like your family. Am I a nuisance, coming so much?'

'No. No, of course you're not. I just wondered if we were being a nuisance, or if you felt you ought to do something about Deirdre. No, I didn't mean that.' She passed a hand over her forehead. 'I shouldn't have said that. It's just that, well, some days get a bit on top of me.'

'Well, ease out, now, and tell me what you've been doing?'

'Oh, what a tempting invitation,' she sighed. 'What's this about your little girl?' she asked suddenly, remembering what

78

Kathy had said.

'Not mine. My sister's. The child is not happy. In fact, the school people have asked me to take her away. I'm collecting her from the train tonight.'

'But where will you take her? Forgive me, but you live at the hospital, don't you?'

'Yes, I can't take her with me to Residents,' he laughed. 'Besides, she is mad about a thing called a recorder, which she blows. She has a friend (or she had) who played what they call Hot Drums. (What *are* Hot Drums?) To be honest, it sounds like good old-fashioned jungle tom-toms to me, but perhaps I'm very square.'

'Yes, but where will she sleep tonight?' Rachel persisted. 'I mean, if you haven't made any arrangements, would you like me to—'

He hesitated before he spoke. There was nothing he would like more. 'A colleague did offer to let her stay with his sister, but she's elderly. I can't think it would be the best plan. But then you, my dear, have your own problems,' he frowned at Rachel. 'I can't think Felicity would lighten your already heavy burdens.'

'It's the day-time,' Rachel frowned. 'It's school holidays and Kathy is at home, and Deirdre, and Neil, but there's Neil's work. He must have quiet for that. Oh, if only there was an older person there, just to keep

79

an eye on everybody and to see the meals were ready on time, then I'd love to have your Felicity. It isn't as if we hadn't got the room to spare and Kathy would be some sort of companionship for her.'

He was silent. He wanted so madly for Felicity to go to that wholesome atmosphere where Rachel was. 'You say if there were an older person there, to cook and generally look after them all?'

'I couldn't afford one, honestly,' Rachel said regretfully.

'Well, my dear, I know that, but I was wondering – you set me thinking, and there is something you could do to help me, as well as have Felicity, I mean. And it might be the answer all round.'

Unlike Kathy, she didn't rush in and promise anything. She quietly waited to hear what he had to say.

'There is an old patient, a bit of a problem,' he frowned. 'I know I should leave it to our Almoner's department, but I know old Mrs Pym so well, and she's very proud, and it's a real disaster for her. She's being turned out of her little cottage and she honestly can't afford it and she has nowhere to go. She's wiry and strong. She would work if you gave her a roof over her head.'

He looked at Rachel, holding his breath. Who would want someone else's teen-ager when they had one of their own? Who would want someone else's old grandmother, taken on trust that she was strong enough, willing enough to work for her board?

She turned suddenly, her face lighting up into that glorious smile. 'Yes, I'll do it – I think it's a perfectly splendid idea,' she beamed. 'Never mind if she can't do much – she'll be there, to fetch me if I'm needed. It's too much to expect Deirdre to be able to put something white on the end of a broom and get to the window and wave it outside, to catch my eye. In real emergency, she might not even remember that time-honoured arrangement. Yes, I like this idea of yours, Dr Ingram.'

'So do I. Well, presuming our Mrs Pym agrees, and presuming Felicity doesn't take against the idea, if you have Mrs Pym and Felicity with you, and I keep coming to visit them to see how they're getting along, and to check that with three kittens, a cat and a dog, too, you're still sane, presumably we could let our back hair down and be madly informal and use first names, what do you think?'

That made her laugh. 'It's Boyd,' he said. 'Let's hear you say it.'

'Boyd,' she repeated obligingly, but nobody else had ever said it like that. She caressed the name before she let it go, as if she were going to sing it. 'And I'm Rachel.'

'I know,' he said. Didn't he know! Warning bells kept ringing in his head. Now was the

81

time to go away before he got too involved. But he couldn't.

They winged their way up the last hill and then down into Astonmore. Rachel directed him to The Gift Shop. 'Who'll be there if the boss is in Birmingham?' he wanted to know, and she said, 'Oh, just the girl who serves in the shop. She's very nice. She's good for the job really. Here we are. Oh, we must stop and look in the window. I want to show you some of the things Deirdre makes.'

They stood companionably at the window, while Rachel pointed out a pink gingham elephant five inches high, and an idiot clown whose amiable face was one broad smile; a small blue fur bear and any number of Mexican hats, whose tiny crowns held thimbles, and the brims hid flannel leaves filled with needles.

A red roadster skimmed by, slowed down for the driver to inspect them, and then quietly purred away. The driver was a pretty girl with a petulant mouth and square sun glasses. Her golden hair streamed out behind, from under the tiny head square, and she wore a very thick sweater with a giant roll collar that could be heightened until it was a hood.

Her companion said, 'Lucille Stevens, what are you up to now? You look like the cat that got the canary and has just made a satisfying meal.'

'Johnny, don't be naughty, darling. I'm not such thing. I just want to make a teensy telephone call.'

She telephoned to the hospital and was lucky enough to find Dr Thora Fenton just about to go home.

'Oh, Thora darling, I'm so glad I was able to catch you like this,' she said.

Thora was guarded in her reply. She could just imagine Lucille, about to impart some tit-bit of gossip before she came to the point and announced what particular trouble she was in. Lucille usually ran a pink tongue over her lips when she began to speak. Thora believed there was nobody who could irritate her more, yet it was always worth her while to keep Lucille out of trouble.

Today was no exception. 'Darling, I just drove past the Gift Shop in Astonmore and I saw someone looking into the window.'

Thora said, 'Go on,' and waited.

'Didn't you tell me, Thora darling, that you were going around with that enigmatic Dr Ingram?'

Thora drew her breath in sharply. 'What if I did? What has he to do with the person you saw in Astonmore?'

'Well, of course I could be wrong,' Lucille said, thinking. 'I was driving Johnny's car and I was a bit worried because, as you probably know – did I tell you? I can't remember – I've had my licence endorsed again. Well, it wasn't my fault. Kick a dog when he's down. You know what these policemen are like! Well, darling, it's no good roaring at me – of course I'm worried about it. That was why perhaps I made a mistake about this person I saw. Only he was tall, just like Boyd Ingram, and a bit stooping, and not very smartly dressed, only somehow, come to think of it, he was more human than Boyd Ingram. You know, laughing with this girl, instead of being the old sobersides you always say he is.'

There was an edge to Thora's voice as she answered: 'Well, *was* it Boyd Ingram, dear, or wasn't it? Because if it wasn't, let's not bother ourselves about it, and discuss your latest scrape instead, shall we?'

Lucille said hastily, 'Well, I think it was.'

'What was the girl like, or didn't you notice?'

'Thora, darling, you sound really horrid, and I'm only doing this for your benefit. Well, I thought you'd like to know. What I mean is, if you *do* want him, I thought you ought to know.'

Thora said, 'How I do loathe those people who rush to tell one there's something they think one ought to know. How long ago did all this happen?'

'It's happening now, darling,' Lucille said maddeningly. 'I can see them, across the street.'

Thora caught her breath. 'All right,

describe the girl.' She added, after a minute, 'That's if you really aren't sure it's Boyd Ingram.'

'Oh, but I am. I mean, he's not laughing at the moment, and you can tell, can't you? She's got brown hair, all pulled back in a bun, and a ghastly dreary jacket and skirt that I wouldn't be seen dead in. How do these shabby girls manage it? He's positively drooling over her! Oh, now they're getting parcels out of the car.'

It was that Roberts woman, Thora told herself, with such an upflow of anger that her face felt as if it was going all tight and bloated and would burst. 'Can you see the car number?' she managed to ask.

'Oh, yes, I can see *that!*' Lucille said, obligingly rattling it off. 'You *are* pleased I telephoned you, aren't you? I can tell you are!'

'Oh, yes, I'm pleased all right,' Thora said, 'and now I must go. There are rather a lot of things I have to attend to.'

'Oh, Thora darling?' Lucille wailed, so Thora waited. Lucille said in her breathless little-girl voice, 'Are you going to show me how glad you are that I phoned you?'

'How much?' Thora said wearily.

'How did you guess?' Lucille cried delightedly. 'Yes, it is a little bill some beastly shop is pressing for, but only a teensy one. I just had to have a new dress to go out with

85

Johnny because he's so particular.'

'How much?' Thora repeated, but when Lucille showed no signs of admitting the price she was in debt, Thora snapped, 'I really can't stop – send the bill to me and I'll settle it,' and she slammed down the receiver into its cradle, and leaned back to the wall, her breath coming so fast she thought she was going to be ill.

That Roberts woman! So *that* was where Boyd vanished to, in every bit of free time he got! That house in Endell Street!

Chapter Four

Mrs Pym was a small woman, with fine brittle-looking bones showing through her skin, and an anxious smile. But since she had got over her bout of bronchitis in hospital, she had got back her old wiriness again and was very cross with herself for being ill.

'Such a silly thing to do, doctor, and now I've lost all those nice jobs I had. Three such nice ladies employed me, and it made a change going out to their houses. No, don't say I'm too old to go scrubbing because I'd only do it in my own little place if I didn't have to do it for anyone else, and they pay me for it, so where's the sense of it all?'

Boyd Ingram told her of the new job he had lined up for her. 'It's rather a delicate situation,' he said.

'Oh, yes?' she said. She liked delicate situations. Gossip was the breath of life to her, and other people's lives were always so much more interesting than her own.

'I want you to go and live in this house. Well, you told me you couldn't afford the rent and you'd had your notice, didn't you?'

'Not if I could find the rent,' she snapped,

spiritedly. 'They can't put me out because it's all my own furniture.'

He sighed. It was going to be like that, was it? How could he tell her that quite apart from being able to afford the rent, by going out in all weathers charring, there was also the rumour that the whole of the block of small houses was going to be pulled down to make way for a supermarket? He decided to forget about that aspect.

'Yes, well, if that's the case, then I'm afraid you won't be able to help me. But I expect I can find someone else.'

'You tell me about it, doctor, and perhaps I shall be able to force myself to go and do what you want, just to please you,' she said.

So he told her briefly about Rachel, who was either a widow or who had a husband away somewhere. 'I don't know her well enough to venture to ask her,' he said quickly, forestalling Mrs Pym's query, 'and the family shy away from the subject. But she's called Mrs Roberts. No, no, not like that at all,' he said hastily, as the worldly Mrs Pym looked knowing. 'Anyway, there is a young man, her cousin, who was blinded in an accident, and her sister who is in a wheelchair through the same accident, and there is her other cousin who is only fifteen.'

'Ah, what a shame,' Mrs Pym said, and shed a few pious tears.

'And there is also a girl of thirteen – my

ward – who will be there temporarily,' he added severely, 'and she is a handful, to say the least, and doesn't merit your tears,' so Mrs Pym dried her eyes.

He took Mrs Pym over early the next morning. He felt he should give her time to settle in before he delivered Felicity from the Barnsley's house in Princes Willow, a village near the sea.

He took Rachel with him to pick up the girl. 'It's really very good of you to have her,' he said gratefully.

Rachel said, 'Oh, no, Boyd, not really. From what you told me about her, I remembered my own childhood. My people were split up, and all the time I felt as if it would have been much better if I hadn't been born. They weren't together much. My father was away at sea–'

'Like your husband?' he ventured, very quickly.

There was an infinitesimal pause, then she went on without answering the question. 'But when my father did come home, he and my mother weren't friends for long. My father died in a foreign port, and my mother was run over, here in England. There didn't seem much sense to any of it. The house we're now in was let. I went to live with Neil's parents until they died. Then when his house became empty we came here, because Neil got a job in Oddenport, and

Deirdre needed sea air. Well, it's near enough to the sea to get there easily,' she said hastily. 'I thought it was tidier and less trouble to live in it than to sell it and buy another one somewhere else, right on the coast perhaps.'

It hadn't answered his question about her husband, nor how she had met her husband or why she had gone on living here. Neil and Deirdre could very well have gone into digs, he thought, frowning.

'And Kathy? How long has she been with you?'

'Oh, Kathy!' She laughed. 'Kathy invited herself over one day and wouldn't leave, poor scrap. She was ten. She said she liked my cooking.'

'But what did her parents say?' He couldn't follow this tangled family web. Not so long ago he had thought the driver in the car in which Deirdre had been injured, had been Rachel's husband, but never had he lost the idea that Rachel's husband was a sailor. He couldn't think who had put it there.

'Kathy's parents were dead. A neighbour was looking after her. So it was in a way rather natural that she should come to us, even if we are only distantly related.'

Distantly related. Was that how she referred to inlaws? Well, he supposed that that was all right. But it was odd. 'Where was Kathy's brother then?' he asked easily, working all the pieces together. Kathy Roberts, Rachel Roberts, and her husband ... who?

She supplied his name unthinkingly. 'Charlie? Did she tell you about him?'

'I can't think who first told me about him,' he said honestly. 'Do you mind, Rachel?'

She hesitated, then she said abruptly, 'Yes, I do mind. I don't want to talk about him.'

'I'm sorry, my dear. It was brutish of me. But I did want it all sorted out in my mind. Well, if Felicity asks questions, just tell her pretty sharply to shut up. She might, you know! She's an awful girl. What they did at that school to teach her manners I can't think, but if they tried to do anything, they certainly failed. The first thing she'll ask you, I guarantee, is "Where's your husband?" So be ready for it.'

Quite unexpectedly Rachel laughed. Quietly, it's true, but her laughter, after her abruptness and refusal to talk about Charlie Roberts, puzzled him. He finally decided that she was also in sympathy with his niece, as well as with Kathy Roberts.

Princes Willow was a picture postcard village by the sea. Professor Barnsley often said cynically that Nature had provided for their preservation. It would have been mightily inconvenient for any planner to try to commercialise the place, but artists liked to come there and paint. There was an artist there now, painting the professor's cottage, much to the annoyance of the elderly lady who had her skirt tucked up, a coarse apron on, and gigantic gardening gloves and a terrible broad-brimmed hat. She was snipping off the old dead blossoms. The artist had put Miss Harriet faithfully in his picture, and she blended.

The garden was crammed with blooms. The cottage, overlapping wood and local stone, was covered with ramblers, and behind it, in the distance, the sea glittered, on this fine day, a raw improbable blue. The artist was leaving the sea alone. He had a couple of inches of it in the left hand corner, with a tiny white sail on it, as if in apology. His picture was saying that this old stone cottage and its owner were cocking a snoot at Time and the elements. It would have looked equally beautiful with or without the sea. Trees were a wind break to one side, the wide arm of the cliff the other.

Rachel said, 'Oh, Boyd, how lovely to live here,' and she just looked at it.

He wanted to agree with her. He had stayed in this cottage, with the professor, in the past. Inside it was enchanting; all whitewashed walls and bits of copper and shining brass, and Waterford glass in little windows, and old, old wood furniture, all antique, bits picked up at sales and put in corners where they looked as if they belonged. Miss Harriet made wool rugs and knitted her own blankets and quilts. There was a sense of peace here. Pumped-up lamps giving a very good light to read the many books by. And flowers everywhere.

Miss Harriet looked up and saw them. She evinced no great pleasure, Rachel was quick to see.

'Hah! Dr Ingram!' was her way of greeting him. 'I trust you've come to take your girl away.'

'Oh, dear,' Boyd murmured and glanced at Rachel. Sympathy was in Rachel's eyes. She had had this sort of greeting in the case of Kathy, when neighbours had taken the girl in on occasion.

'Never mind,' Rachel murmured softly, as he stood back to let her go into the open gate. 'It wasn't your fault.'

Miss Harriet said tartly, 'She has broken a piece of my best Waterford glass, two pieces of porcelain which I set her to dust, and she lcft the larder door open and the cats got in and ate all the food or spoiled it. Also she sulks. Never could abide a person who sulked!'

Rachel glanced at Boyd. The old look was settling over his face; a guarded look, where he could retire behind it and feel hurt because someone had been harsh in criticism of his own. Well, she understood that, too. She herself always bristled when anyone outside the family criticized Kathy. She listened to Boyd making graceful and sincere apologies and promising to make the damage good, and then she spotted Felicity.

Boyd spotted Felicity at the same time. She was standing half-hidden by the curtain which was looped back from the top of an archway leading to the stairs. The staircase in this cottage had no hand-rails; it went up wedged between two walls. Felicity came out from the curtain with a theatrical gesture which reminded Rachel of what Boyd had said about the mother – an actress.

Boyd said, 'Good grief! Take that stuff off your face at once! Where did you get it, anyway?'

Rachel murmured, 'She's only dressing up,' but Boyd didn't listen. He looked so unexpectedly angry, yet to Rachel's eyes it was rather funny, pathetically funny. The girl was extremely pretty in a dark way, and she had piled her black hair under a mantilla. Over her dress she wore, in provocative fashion, a colourful shawl, and in her strong white teeth she held a rose. A Spanish dancer, not just depending on the frightfully applied make-up, but something in the way she looked and stood. If the mother was an actress, then she could be happy that her daughter had inherited the gift.

Neither Boyd nor Miss Harriet were happy. Miss Harriet said, 'Why, disgraceful girl, that's the shawl off my piano! Put it back at once, do! And have you cut one of my best red roses?'

Felicity threw both on the floor and thudded up the stairs in floods of tears. Boyd's anger crumpled into utter dismay, and Miss Harriet stormed about the place, washing after her gardening, so that she could, as she said, replace the shawl and put the place to rights.

'I'm Rachel Roberts. She's going to stay with me, Miss Harriet,' Rachel said gently, because Boyd seemed too upset to remember to introduce her. 'Perhaps you could tell me a few things about what she likes to eat, and so on.'

'You're having her?' Miss Harriet snapped, looking at Rachel for the first time. 'More fool you! You'll wish you'd never been born.'

Rachel said to Boyd, 'I think I'll go up to her,' which just forestalled his own leaping at the stairs, four at a time. 'You stay here with Miss Harriet.'

She found Felicity sobbing noisily on the bed in a tiny room that had a wonderful view of the sea.

She stood beside the bed. There wasn't room for anything else but one person to stand there, but it was a charming room for a young person. At least, it would have been,

Rachel thought, if all of Felicity's things hadn't been strewn everywhere. There were too many shoes blocking the way for Rachel to even get to the little round window and peep down at the shore, which she would have liked to do. What a pretty little house!

She caught herself up severely from her yearnings. They kept bursting through too often, since she had met Boyd Ingram in the hairdressers that day, which was ridiculous, since he was about to be engaged to Dr Fenton. Well, wouldn't one expect that sort of alliance? They were of an age, and the same background.

She sighed and turned to Felicity, who had stopped sobbing and was regarding her slyly through opened fingers. There were so many things she could say to this girl. Rachel thought of them, and discarded them one by one. At last, she said, 'You did that rather well. It was quite obvious to me that you were being the Rhythm of the Flamenco, or something similar!'

Felicity lowered her hand and uncovered her face, streaked with tears and running mascara. 'Go on, say I'm too young for make-up.'

'Well, so you are, but who's talking about make-up? Stage make-up's all right if you're concentrating on acting, which I imagine you were. By the way, have you got a proper make-up box?'

Felicity asked warily, 'Why?'

Rachel shrugged. 'I thought we might stage some more of these acts of yours, to see what you can do. Please yourself.'

'You mean you wouldn't *mind?*'

'No, with reservations,' Rachel said coolly.

'Oh, those! I thought there'd be a catch in it,' Felicity growled.

'There's always something,' Rachel agreed. 'Because it can't be managed to let one person have all her own way. It just doesn't work. In my house, people have to be *sensible.*'

Felicity said, 'That's a new one, but it's all the same. Grown-ups use different words, but they all have the same idea. If you're not adult then you're supposed to shut up.'

'Is that bad?' Rachel asked, with her blazing smile. All her sympathies were going out to this very pretty girl who was her own enemy.

Felicity got up and jumped off the bed, but as there was so little room, she had to spoil the effect by getting back on to the bed. But she knelt on it, which brought her almost to Rachel's height, and she said fiercely, 'Listen, I don't know what my uncle's going to pay you for having me, but let's get this straight. All right, I'm only thirteen, but I've been expelled from four schools, just because I *won't* shut up, and do you know why I won't shut up? Because I've got intelligence, more than a lot of grown-ups, and I reckon that the young ought to be heard because they've got new and fresh ideas, and just because you're young, it doesn't mean you've got to sit and be quiet and do as you're told. Do you know what? Grown-ups make me sick!'

She held her breath and listened, but Boyd was talking to Miss Harriet below, not storming up the stairs to deliver six of the best where she sat down, as he had done last time. That had been when her mother had had a row with him. That had been bad. Boyd and her mother had looked at each other as if they had honestly hated each other.

She brought her frightened thoughts back from that memory, uncomfortably aware that it had been her fault. But it hadn't been her fault that her mother had quarrelled like that with her father before he had died. She regarded Rachel with care. Was this going to be a chicken adult, sitting on the fence hoping for peace and quiet? Or a shouting angry adult like the stupid old woman downstairs, angry at having her prissy neat place messed up for a few days? Felicity was uncomfortably aware that she didn't know how Rachel was going to turn out, but that inevitably Rachel would come out on top.

Rachel looked kindly at her. 'You know, it's remarkable! I can't believe it! *I* used to talk like that at your age! I know just how you feel – I can remember! Honestly! But the awful thing is, you see, one can't just stay young and put the world to rights. You seem to grow up so quickly before you've had time to do anything. And when you're grown up you get responsibilities and forget about all the things you wanted to do. I wanted revolution.'

Felicity's eyes lit. 'Me, too! Did you really?'

'Yes, and abolishing all schools–'

'Well, no, not all schools,' Felicity said quickly. 'Not drama schools, I mean. They're good. They're not to be touched.'

'Oh, you're not a real rebel then,' Rachel admonished her. 'You must go all the way or not at all. I mean, it's not the thing to pick and choose.'

'You're getting at me!' Felicity stormed.

'Yes, I used to fall back on that line too, when I was losing,' Rachel sighed. 'Isn't it *funny?* Funny-peculiar, I mean. And now look at me! It was because my parents used to fight, so, I suppose.'

'They did?' Felicity unwillingly forgot her battle for the moment. 'What happened? Did you run away?'

'I was going to,' Rachel admitted thoughtfully. 'Only Neil, my cousin, said that was chicken, and while I was thinking about it, my father died, abroad, and soon after that, my mother was run over.'

Felicity held her breath and waited.

'Neil's parents took me in, because there was nobody else, and they were decent, and anyway, it knocked me sideways a bit, to lose both my parents.' She regarded Felicity thoughtfully. Again there were so many things to say and so many ways of saying them, but Felicity wouldn't want to hear them, so she said casually, 'I mean, I'm not superstitious, but it almost seemed as if, well, I was being warned, if you see what I mean, to go easy for a while. I mean, losing both your parents like that.'

Felicity wriggled uncomfortably.

'Are we going to this Neil person's place, then?' she demanded.

'No, my own house. But Neil is there. He was in a road accident. He can't see.' She drew a sharp breath, wanting badly to say something like 'And no-one, nobody at all, is to worry him or make a row', but that would be asking for trouble. 'He's one of those blind people who can do things. Things like laying the table and typing his own newspaper stuff (he's a journalist) and taking out his own mail. He won't even have our dog go with him, and he almost never falls over the cat and the kittens. You *are* a cat-lover, I hope?' she said fiercely, pretending not to have noticed the way Felicity's face lit at the mention of the cat and kittens.

'Super – yes, I am! How many?' Felicity demanded eagerly.

'Oh, three or four, at the moment. There are usually a lot around. Kathy likes them.'

'Who's Kathy?' Felicity asked.

'Someone rather like you, two years older. No parents. Loathes everyone and everything if it means doing as she's told,' Rachel smiled.

When Boyd came cautiously up the stairs, he heard Rachel say, 'That's right, sling 'em in this case. You're right up to time. Didn't think you'd do it. It's quicker than Kathy can pack, actually, and she's held the record, so far.'

He heard Felicity say, 'Why didn't you tell me to mind and not crease everything? They did at school.'

'That's part of their job. It's not mine. I've only undertaken to provide you with a roof over your head, good food, not let you wear things that aren't aired, or get soaked too often in the rain, and keep everyone in my home from driving each other insane. All right? Let's get moving, then.'

Boyd turned, a tender smile on is face, and hurried downstairs again, before they realized that he had heard anything. That was Rachel at her best! The first time he had witnessed her in action, but he had rather expected a slick performance, tackling any problem, even one as big as this!

He stowed his niece and her luggage in the car, and stood for a moment, with Rachel's admirable help, smoothing down Miss Harriet and promising to make good the damage Felicity had done. Then they turned to go into the car too, but Rachel paused to look at the sea.

'It's such a beautiful village,' she murmured. 'I know we live near enough to have come here often, but it's always the way when there isn't a direct bus route and you haven't a car – somehow one just doesn't make the effort. I wish I had.'

'So do I,' Boyd said. 'And I *have* a car, but I've never been here to enjoy the village, only to dine with my old friend and his sister, and very rarely at that. I've an idea – why don't we spend the day here. Now! Well, what's there to rush for?'

Rachel looked surprised and laughed up at him. 'A little matter of the hospital, I suppose, and my job! You forgot it wasn't the week-end, didn't you?'

'Well, then, the week-end, why don't we come on Saturday? We could bring the rest of the family – surely? Well, if Neil won't come, we could give Deirdre a treat, couldn't we?'

Rachel looked consideringly at him. 'You've forgotten something else, haven't you? Dr Fenton. I'm sure she's arranged something for Saturday. I believe I heard her mention it when she made a hair appointment for late Friday.'

And that seemed to settle that. His smile ebbed away, and Rachel became brisk, and turned her back on the shore and climbed into the car, over the box containing the guitar and the concertina, and the big cardboard box with the theatrical costumes, and all the other paraphernalia that it hadn't been possible to wedge into the three big cases holding Felicity's worldly goods. Felicity looked at her sharply, those wide eyes holding a good deal of curiosity.

'What were you talking about?' she demanded. 'Out there just now. Me?'

'No, my dear, oddly enough we were talking about Princes Willow. When you get too old to have time to change the world, you suddenly discover that you like some of it as it is. I like this village.'

'Ugh!' Felicity said, expressively. 'Hope I never get like that. Well, I won't, of course. You like Uncle Boyd, don't you?'

As Boyd was sitting at the wheel, trying with one hand to drive in a straight line up the narrow hill out of Princes Willow and to steady a great box of stuff propped against the front seat, Rachel wished that Felicity hadn't asked that question.

She said, in a non-committal voice, 'I imagine everybody likes your Uncle Boyd.'

'Now that's a rotten grown-up way of

getting out of answering the question,' Felicity exploded. 'I didn't think you'd be like that. Oh!' she said suddenly, and leaned forward to grab at Rachel's left hand. 'I say, you're married. I didn't notice that ring before. Why didn't you say so?'

'I thought perhaps Miss Harriet would have spoken of me.'

'She did. She calls you *that Rachel Arden.*'

'Oh, well, some elderly people don't remember very easily the new name. I thought she would have referred to me as Mrs Roberts.'

Felicity sensed a certain amount of tension in the car, and said shortly, 'No, she never did. She just said she couldn't imagine why that Rachel Arden was fool enough to take on someone like me and that there must be something in it that she hadn't had time to see. She said she'd get round to it, when she was quiet.'

There was a smothered sound from Boyd, echoed by Rachel, and then Rachel felt she ought to show some indignation, so she remarked, 'I suppose you upset poor Miss Barnsley so much by the bad things you did, that she forgot to let her thoughts remain silent. I get like that sometimes.'

'What, when you have fights with your husband? You do fight with him, I bet you do! You're a fighty sort of person but I like you.'

'That will *do,* Felicity,' Boyd put in from the front seat.

'You don't mind what I say, do you?' Felicity demanded of Rachel.

'Not so far, but if I do, you may rest assured I'll tell you. Boyd, I've just remembered I would like to stop for some extra groceries. Have you time?'

He said he had, and his eyes looked at her in the driving mirror. She was conscious of a little glow. It was so domesticated and nice and friendly, all of a sudden; surrounded by luggage, both rising to correct Boyd's niece, and making arrangements to stop for eggs and things. She caught herself up suddenly. Don't live in a fool's paradise! Remember Dr Fenton! She has the opportunity, the will and the prior claim...

'Who will be at your house when we get there?' Felicity asked all of a sudden. 'This Kathy person?'

'Yes, she'll be there. She'll help you settle in, if you like. I've put your room next to hers.'

'Well, if I like her, that'll be all right, but if I hate her, don't blame me if we throw things and bang on the wall at each other, because that's what I do.'

'Then you'd better make up your mind to change your ways,' Rachel said cheerfully, 'because Neil is blind and everyone gives in to him and it has to be quiet while he's

105

working. Your unclc will agree, I'm sure.'

Boyd did, in no uncertain terms. He did it so heavily that Rachel felt bound to change the subject before Felicity forgot the truce she had offered.

'There is also an elderly person who looks after things.'

'A housekeeper? Why don't you call her that?' Felicity said.

'Nothing so grand, I'm afraid. She's an old patient of your uncle's who needs a roof over her head and she's agreed to do a certain amount of odd jobs and giving an eye to the place while I'm at work. I'm in the reception desk of a hairdressing salon.'

Boyd wished Rachel hadn't put it like that. He knew Felicity only too well. Those schools her mother had chosen had brought her up as a little snob.

He was very much surprised, therefore, to hear Felicity express satisfaction. 'Oh, no maids in uniform? Good-o. They make me sick. We have them at school. Do we eat in the kitchen? I'd like that. Some people do and it looks fun. You see them when you go by in a train at night.'

Rachel looked sharply at Felicity, infinite kindness and tenderness in her face. Boyd noticed the look. Loneliness, the utter need for a family background was partly Felicity's trouble, he was sure. A rush of gratitude for Rachel and her family sped over him. He couldn't get to the house in Endell Street fast enough, to see Felicity settled in.

Neil was pottering about when they arrived. Deirdre was sewing and paused to greet the newcomer. Mrs Pym complained, 'This young man insists on making tea, doctor, dear, and you didn't tell me that I'd have someone else doing things in my kitchen.'

Rachel looked across the room at Boyd. 'Mrs Pym,' she said quickly, 'I do need your help rather specially here,' and she began to take the cases upstairs, the little woman at the other end. Give Mrs Pym something to drag or push, and she felt she was doing a worthwhile job.

Upstairs, she said, 'Oh, dear, I'm sorry you're upset. I forgot to tell you about Neil. He's getting about so nicely without his sight but for some reason it's terribly important to let him get tea. I don't know why. I suppose he feels it's a challenge to handle a tea kettle of boiling water–'

'He'll scald himself one of these days, that's what he'll do!' Mrs Pym said, betraying anxiety on that score as her one point at issue.

'No, I don't think so, if you don't come on him suddenly. He never interferes with any other form of cooking, and you know, there are so many things we need you to do in this rather rambling house, that can't be done

107

without sight, don't you see?'

It was exhausting, mollifying Mrs Pym, who was determined to pay back everything about this satisfying new life the doctor had placed before her, and was jealous of anyone like Neil taking any opportunity from her, however small. 'See, you don't understand, dear, I've only been in this house one day, and I know it's just what I wanted, already. It's the family, d'you see? Being with people. I never knew I missed people so much when I was on my own. I wouldn't like to go back to it now.'

'You hold your horses. You haven't seen the doctor's young niece in action, yet,' Rachel warned her, smiling broadly.

'It don't matter, dear, not anything matters. We shall come about, but I just want to feel I'm pulling my weight, doing things, and we shall all be happy and cosy. Especially the doctor. He likes being here, don't he? The minute he got in, he sat down as if he was used to it, and the kittens all ran up his arm and he didn't seem to mind. I couldn't help noticing that. I said to myself, now which one of these young ladies is he interested in? A pity you've got a husband, dear, or I would have thought–'

'Here comes the girls,' Rachel broke in. She had been warned by Boyd that little Mrs Pym would be very inquisitive. Perhaps, as the little woman said, it was only because she did live such a lonely life. But it mustn't be allowed to go too far!

She went out to the landing. Kathy was bringing Felicity up. One look at the young people's faces, and Rachel's heart sank. They didn't like each other.

She said to them, 'Is Neil all right? He looked rather pale, I thought. If he's got one of his headaches–'

'He got into a temper. That Hazel Otty came in from next door,' Kathy snapped.

'Oh, dear,' Rachel sighed. 'What did she want?'

'To worry him, about not being able to "talk" to him, which means she wanted a petting party–'

'Oh, Kathy, stop it,' Rachel said crossly. It was one thing to let Kathy say what she wanted to, but quite another for these slang expressions that upset Neil if he heard them. 'Besides, that isn't true.'

'Oh, isn't it,' Kathy retorted. 'She's been jigging about doing the latest dance steps and wouldn't let him work. Honestly, I don't know how she gets away with it. You won't let me bother him!'

'And I wouldn't have let her bother him if I'd been here,' Rachel retorted, going after Felicity to see if her room met with her approval.

'She plays the piano!' Felicity said, nodding to where Kathy had gone into her room and slammed the door. 'You didn't tell me!'

'Does it matter, or do you mean you're pleased?' Rachel asked.

'I loathe the piano,' Felicity said.

'Then you've got company. Everyone else in this house loathes it when Kathy plays. But I should have thought you two could come to terms. You with your instruments and Kathy accompanying you.'

'She doesn't want to. She wants to be star performer. And another thing – she's ignorant. She doesn't know that stringed instruments originated in – oh, centuries ago. She doesn't know about the mandolins the minstrels played, and the lute and lyre and all the others. She just thinks an electric guitar was something invented by pop groups and that the piano is the only classical form of music. She's very ignorant.'

'We'll have to get together on this,' Rachel said faintly, astonished that Felicity should have any such knowledge herself. One eye on the time, for going in to her job, she hurried downstairs. Today it would have to be a ham sandwich for her, although she had left a casserole in the oven for the others, and Mrs Pym with instructions how to serve it.

Neil said to her after Boyd had left, 'Rachel, I'd like to talk to you about Hazel, when you've a minute. I know you're in a

110

rush now, so don't worry. But if you've got just the odd minute, I wish you'd brief me about what Felicity is like.'

'Didn't Dr Ingram tell you? I thought you would have asked him.'

'He can't describe people like you,' Neil said.

'Well, I notice she's almost as tall as Kathy, but rather willowy with it. As you know, she's only thirteen, but she's read up a lot of stuff about having a revolution and all that, but oddly she's passionate about acting. Her mother, you know.'

'Yes, no doubt she'll tell me all about that, but what does she look like?' and he sounded distracted, which he hadn't done for some time.

'She's dark. So dark that she was able to make up like a Spanish dancer for our benefit. Dark eyes, dark hair, a rich golden sort of skin. Nice teeth, but a rather full mouth. Oh, dear,' Rachel said.

'Why did you say "oh dear"?' Neil asked quickly.

'Just rueful. She's so pretty and bold looking. Kathy won't like that. They don't like each other, as it is. Perhaps that's why.'

'Are we alone?' Neil asked abruptly.

'Yes. And Mrs Pym's banging about in the kitchen, as you can hear. Did you want to talk about something, my dear?' She meant Hazel next door, but refrained from saying so from delicacy. Neil was so sensitive.

He hesitated. 'Yes, I do, mainly about what we do about, well, the husband.' He hesitated again. 'First, I have to ask a blunt question, and I don't know how to. You won't like it, Rachel. This Dr Ingram, you like him rather, don't you?'

She hesitated too long to be able to deny it.

'It won't do me any good, Neil,' she said at last. 'Let's forget it.'

'He likes you,' Neil offered. 'Rachel, you can't go through life pretending to be happy. Oh, I know you make a good pretence of it, but do you think I don't *know?* Just because I can't see? There are times when I want to go around kicking people because of the present situation.'

'I'm not complaining, Neil,' she said at last. 'Now, my dear, since you've raised that point, we'd better decide what we're going to say, because Felicity's already starting asking questions.'

'Just refuse to talk about Charlie Roberts,' Neil said coldly. 'You don't have to satisfy that brat about any of it. Oh, and you really should tell Kathy what to say – not that we've any guarantee that she'll abide by it, but we must try.'

Rachel nodded, as if he could see. 'Sometimes I wonder if I did the right thing there, Neil. But there wasn't any other way,

112

was there?' she sighed.

'I often wonder,' Neil said bluntly. 'It would seem that a married woman has more chances than a single one, but I think we'll regret it, one day. Oh, I know you said you didn't care, having been hurt once. I'm beginning to know what you felt like then. But I wonder if it lasts? I wonder what I shall feel like if I find you've got over that first business, and really feel serious about some other chap. Well, you're hardly free, are you?'

'I could tell him all about it,' she protested.

'Would he feel the same?' Neil argued. 'I don't think I would, if I were the chap.'

'Well, anyway, if it's Boyd Ingram you're thinking I'm getting worked up about, then you're wrong, Neil,' she said vigorously. 'And he isn't that way about me, either. It's that Dr Fenton. You should just see the way he runs when she crooks her little finger to him.'

'You'll soon be telling me there's a pull somewhere,' Neil commented. 'A place in Harley Street, or a private nursing home for him, as a prize for taking her off the family's hands. Well, if she looks like she sounds, her family would need to do something!' His lips twitched, and Rachel chuckled.

'Neil, you *are* the limit! You're right, of course. Me, I can't stand her. But I believe she's a very good doctor.'

'Deirdre doesn't think so,' he commented.

'Neil, I must rush. Look at the time!' They neither of them noticed her wording of that. He felt with sensitive finger-tips over his special watch and agreed with her that she should hurry. 'And think it over what we must say about Charlie Roberts,' he said again.

She grabbed up her coat, flinging it on as she went out. She had forgotten her sandwich lunch. Neil fretted to find the door to go after her, and then wondered what he could do if he did call her back. He supposed she would send out for a sandwich to have with her tea, later.

Dr Fenton's appointment was the first for Raoul after he came back from lunch. It was a long appointment. She was having a manicure and her rather heavy brows plucked as well. And a facial, Rachel saw with surprise.

Not long after that, Boyd telephoned. 'Rachel, can you tell me what time Dr Fenton's appointment is?' and he sounded bothered. She read it out of the book to him, leaving out the personal details. No woman wanted her man to know what she had done at the hairdresser's.

'She tells me I'm supposed to be calling for her but I didn't know it was today. Are you sure it is?'

Rachel confirmed it, firmly. 'Three o'clock

until five.'

'Why is it such a long appointment? How can it take so long for a woman to have her hair washed and dried?'

That made her chuckle. 'It's rather a practical way of putting it, isn't it? Actually, it's a lot more than that, and people with long hair take longer to dry than those with short hair.'

'Well, you should know,' he said, thinking of her hair and the way it curled underneath, and the way it swung when she walked. It shone. How many times did she brush it? Clutton was complaining only that morning (as a change from talking about his bank balance) that his wife (when he could get home) always demanded that he brush her hair for her fifty strokes at bedtime. Boyd thought it could be a pleasant task. Especially for someone like Rachel.

After she had put the telephone down, there was nothing to do. It hadn't been such a slack afternoon for a long time. Rachel began to feel hungry and recalled that she hadn't had any lunch.

Madame came out. Rachel said, 'Would you mind terribly if I went out to get a sandwich? I didn't have any lunch. I could have it with my tea.'

Madame wasn't busy, either. She said, 'Run back home, silly girl, and get yourself an egg and milk or something. You can't live

115

on sandwiches.' Then as Rachel half rose in her chair, Madame said, 'No, better still, pop down the road and get a fried egg and bacon lunch. I can be sure you'll have enough then, and you won't run into trouble that'll keep you, which is what will happen if you go back home,' and she smiled broadly.

Madame was right, of course, Rachel had to allow. Heaven knew what was going on between Felicity and Kathy, and Neil might raise another problem about Charlie Roberts.

She sat there eating her bacon and eggs and wondering what she should do. Felicity would ask her questions about the husband: that was obvious. Kathy might blurt out something, too. But then, if she told Boyd about it, it might just get out, and get to Madame's ears, and that was the last thing she wanted. Madame and her passion for married employees was at the root of the trouble, though she didn't know it.

Ten minutes later she was back at her desk. Madame said, 'You'll kill yourself with indigestion, my girl,' but she looked pleased that Rachel hadn't taken advantage and stayed away any longer. She looked as if she were going to settle down for a chat. Sometimes when Madame wasn't too busy she liked to enjoy a grumble about that flighty husband of hers.

But today there was little chance. Dr

Fenton came in, at five to three.

Rachel thought she had never noticed before what cold eyes Dr Fenton had. She looked straight at Rachel as she said good afternoon to Madame, and all the while she was taking off her gloves and casually saying a few things to Madame, and to the girl who was to wash the doctor's hair, Thora Fenton stared coldly at Rachel, until Rachel began to feel rather uncomfortable.

Suddenly Thora Fenton looked away, and smiled warmly as Raoul came out. She followed him in, and Rachel shuddered. What on earth was all that about, she thought?

Madame said nothing, however, so Rachel found something to do, and the afternoon wore on.

A little later on, she was aware of a conversation that had been going on behind her. It was the cubicle in which Thora Fenton was. She had had her shampoo and her manicure. Now Raoul was arranging her hair, setting it with artistry and love. He was really wasted in this job, Rachel thought. Suddenly to her dismay, it was as if that thought had been whipped from her mind and put into the voice of Dr Fenton.

'You're wasted here, Raoul. You know that, don't you?' she said.

Knowing Madame as she did, Rachel looked round for her, and saw her at the end, talking quietly to one of the new girls

117

about the treatment of a wig. This was a new craft that the young ones liked. They worked quickly on menial jobs in the salon, such as sweeping up hair cuttings, taking the towels out for laundering, washing down the basins, so that they could be free to take a turn under Madame's able tuition. Samara York might have originated in East London from mixed parentage, but she knew her craft well, and if she wasn't as artistic as her husband with styling to suit the particular customer, she was an excellent wig-maker and a fine teacher. Engrossed in what she was showing the girl, Rachel doubted if she was really able to hear what Thora was saying to Raoul. There was the constant hum of a dryer, and the splash of water in another cubicle. Only Rachel could hear the destructive line Thora was taking.

'It's no use letting a certain person override you, Raoul,' Dr Fenton said softly. 'You know who I mean, and you have to be realistic. You are outstanding at the work, while someone else (you know who I mean) is merely competent.'

Raoul murmured something. Rachel imagined how he would be looking; vaguely excited, but a little afraid. His wife had the money, not him. She had inherited from her father, who had made it from eel pie stalls, and his three fried fish and chip shops. Madame might be ashamed of her antecedents, but that didn't mean that she didn't regard her father's money with respect and that she would be likely to finance Raoul in London. She wouldn't!

Dr Fenton said, 'Now you think about this. There are openings for a good stylist like you, and there are people who would finance you. Oh, how I hate to see waste, and you really are wasted in this one-eyed hole.'

Again Raoul murmured something, to which she replied, 'Rubbish! Well, of course, I don't want to come between husband and wife. It isn't my place to. It's for you to make the break, for you to kick your way up the ladder. All I'm saying is, you are capable of doing it, amply capable, and if it's money you want, well, I know people who might be interested in the investment.'

Rachel went hot with anger. More sensible men might just take this as a customer's flattery and forget it. Not Raoul. He would bask in it, nurture it, take it to sleep with him, dream about it all day until it became so big that it would burst out in a big quarrel between him and Madame. Rachel flinched from the thought. There had been other quarrels like this in the past, the other girls had told her. That had been why the Madame had insisted on married women only in the salon.

She forgot about it while Dr Fenton was

under the dryer. She remembered it when Boyd arrived to pick Dr Fenton up.

This time he was no longer bashful. He came in confidently and stood talking to Rachel about Felicity, until Dr Fenton came out.

'Don't stand any nonsense with her, will you?' he was saying.

Rachel smiled faintly. 'We've had nonsense already,' she said. 'She doesn't like Kathy.'

'Oh, no! I never heard such rubbish. I'll come over tonight – oh, no, I can't,' he said, nettled, remembering where he was taking Dr Fenton. It was a highbrow concert. He had refused to come in a dinner jacket but he looked very nice in a dark lounge suit. Thora Fenton came out all ready, just as he said that. She caught his nettled frown, and Rachel saw the subtle change in Dr Fenton's face. This, Rachel thought, was going to get increasingly difficult.

Madame came out to take the money personally. She usually did. Thora Fenton greeted Boyd quietly enough, and then suddenly turned to Rachel. 'By the way, Mrs Roberts, is your husband's name Charles?'

Of course, the Madame was all ears. She had often tried to persuade Rachel to talk about that elusive husband. Rachel said stiffly, more aware of Boyd's intent look, 'Yes, it is.'

'Well, don't you want to know how I came

to know that?' she said, teasingly, a broad smile on her face. She felt well-groomed, elegant, happy, and she had done a good job on Raoul. She saw him at work in a salon in London that she would set up for him, exclusively doing her hair and being for ever grateful to her. She loved people to be grateful to her. And she had an in-built suspicion and hatred for people like Madame, who manipulated a group of people so well that they worked happily together and even believed they were happy; Dr Fenton's greatest burden in life was that she couldn't manipulate people in the mass.

She watched Rachel's embarrassment with a curious kind of triumph. She had no real information, just a coincidental meeting and a hunch, but it was worth a trial just for fun, and it appeared to have scored its mark. Rachel said, 'No, Dr Fenton, it doesn't matter.'

'Oh, but it does,' Boyd interposed, displeasure showing in his face. He had built up a notion that Rachel was a widow. He wanted to prove that that was so. It was imperative that Dr Fenton should be wrong. 'How did you come to make such a mistake, Thora, as to think Mrs Roberts' husband is living? She's a widow.'

'No, I don't think so,' Thora murmured. '*Are* you, my dear?'

Rachel looked hunted. She wanted to say

outright so many things, but there was Madame at her elbow, giving this special customer the honour of having her bill made out by the proprietress. 'Oh, I think not,' Madame said quickly, looking sharply at Rachel. 'Mrs Roberts knows my rules. All my pals must have a husband. That is an unbreakable rule; she knows that, don't you, dear?' she said to Rachel.

Rachel nodded. 'That's so, Madame,' she agreed.

'There you are, then,' Dr Fenton said, in a pleased voice. 'I didn't think I'd made a mistake. One meets all sorts in hospital, and this chappie was so handsome – in his naval uniform, too. The first Roberts I'd come across for ages, and I couldn't resist asking if he were related, and he was.' She smiled thoughtfully at Rachel. 'Why didn't you mention that your husband was a patient of mine?'

Madame was looking concerned. 'Oh, dear, what is wrong with him, doctor? Nothing serious, I hope?'

Rachel's heart began to thud, unevenly. Was Dr Fenton making it up, or was there really a naval officer called Charlie Roberts, a patient of hers? She looked at Samara York, and longed to be able to say, I'm sorry, but Dr Fenton is wrong. Whoever this man is, he isn't my husband – I haven't got a husband! But there was this job. Where could she get such another job, with elastic hours, and within sight of home? Not too badly paid, too, because for Madame, Rachel was a find, in that she didn't mind how long overtime she stayed, or what jobs she took on.

And the moment slid by, and the chance was gone, because Dr Fenton said, with a smiling glance at Boyd, 'Nothing terribly serious. The poor chap picked up a "Bug" on his last voyage, and it's brought out a rash on one hand. We'll soon have it cleared up. And it isn't catching,' she assured Madame, who was fluttering round looking anxious.

Boyd looked at Rachel. 'You might have told me,' his look said, but he didn't say it. He had no right. He had slipped into being a friend of the family in a very short time, but that gave him no rights where Rachel was concerned.

'...and he's so handsome,' Thora Fenton was saying to Madame. 'You should ask Mrs Roberts to bring him here, and you'll have all your girls flocking round him in no time.'

Madame smiled thinly. Rachel was quite sure that a handsome husband wouldn't be welcomed here, Madame being a stickler for the 'girls' to keep their minds on their work all the time. If they started flocking round someone else's husband, all her carefully built up plans would crash and Raoul would become shockingly out of hand. But it was no policy of hers to quarrel with a customer! 'We shall see, Dr Fenton,' she said archly, and Thora settled her bill and bore Boyd out of the shop.

Rachel shut her eyes and tried to banish that look on his face, as if he couldn't believe it was true. Yet what had she done? It was no business of his what any husband of hers was or did, and he hadn't asked her. But it was news to her that he had thought her a widow. She had supposed she had implied it, by never speaking of a husband, and dodging away from the subject whenever it got close. And to think that she and Neil had been talking of this subject only today, and hadn't got round to what they should arrange!

If only she could have talked to Neil! They must brief Kathy, and be prepared to face questions from Felicity, before Boyd Ingram had a chance to question Rachel herself. She was quite sure he would.

But who was the man that Dr Fenton had been treating, she asked herself frenziedly. Which man would say he was the husband of Rachel Arden, which man who was a handsome young officer in the Navy would do such a thing? Someone enjoying a joke? Surely not! Rachel flinched from any such new complication.

Madame, having shut the door on them,

said sharply, 'Are you all right, dear?' and when Rachel said she had a headache but that she would be all right, Madame said, 'You have kept that husband of yours rather a secret, come to think of it. Why, dear?'

Rachel summoned her forces and smiled. 'Well, I'm not one to talk about my private business, am I, any more than you are, Madame, and I didn't think you'd be particularly interested.'

Madame's face cleared. 'No, well, that's true, and I've always liked that about you, dear. Most girls are only too ready to waste time in gossip. Still, Dr Fenton did seem so surprised, didn't she?'

Rachel couldn't keep the sharp note out of her voice as she said, 'I can't think why! She hardly knows me.'

Madame looked as if she wanted to say something but changed her mind, and hurried to the back again, to see what the part-time married woman was doing with a double load of soiled towels she was supposed to be putting in the washing machine. Rachel watched her thoughtfully; there was no justice. She herself had been stiff, angry, but Dr Fenton had been all smiles, friendliness and sweet reason. She could see that Dr Ingram had noticed that, as well.

Boyd Ingram, however, had hardly noticed how Thora had treated Rachel. All he could think about was the fact that Rachel was not only married but that her young husband was handsome enough to have interested Thora. Why hadn't Rachel mentioned him? How could Rachel have pottered around her home, so happily, giving confidences about the family to Boyd himself but never mentioning the husband? Sliding away from the subject so that he himself had decided the husband must be dead! And then he remembered the occasion when Rachel had found something amusing in what he had said about the husband. He struggled to recall what it was, and missed what Thora was saying.

'Boyd, dear,' she said again, gently insisting. 'Where are you? Come back!'

'Don't be silly, Thora,' he said, shrugging a little. 'I wasn't away from you. I was listening to you.' It was a rash thing to say but it usually pacified her.

Today he was sorry he had said that. She said, pleased, 'Oh, so you *were* thinking about Rachel Roberts and that handsome young husband! I thought you might. I must say it's odd she never seems to have the need to babble about him, as so many young women do about their husbands. You'd think, with one so handsome, and so devoted to her–'

'*Is* he devoted?' Boyd asked sharply. 'Well, I mean, he doesn't seem to be at the house much.'

'Now how would you know that, Boyd?' she asked, keeping the smile on her face but hating Rachel Roberts.

'Because I'm interested enough in the sister, to go there. I feel something can be done about the girl. I know she's your patient, Thora, but that isn't hysteria.'

This was where they had left off last time, and she had had to hastily give in because he was getting angry about it. She dropped the subject of his visits to the home of Rachel Roberts and said instead, 'If you remember, I did say I thought that girl had something on her mind. I wonder if it's the "bug" he picked up that's worrying her. I suppose I ought to have assured her that it isn't all that important.'

He was pleasantly surprised. 'Now that is kind of you, Thora. I wish you would. Honestly, she had enough to carry on those slim shoulders, without the worry of something the husband caught. I wonder how long he's home for? Do you happen to know?'

'As a matter of fact, he told me he wasn't going to sea any more. He doesn't like being away. Well, he wouldn't, would he?'

She watched his face, but Boyd didn't betray the wave of anger he felt against the mysterious husband of Rachel. Another thought had occurred to him. How would the husband take the arrival of his own niece? And why hadn't Rachel told him the husband would be at home? Did she need the extra money all that much?

'What address did he give?' Boyd asked suddenly.

'Well, bless me, I can't remember,' Thora said comfortably.

'But you must know whether it was Endell Street or not,' Boyd said.

'Are you worried in case there should be trouble in the nest of your special patient, then?' she teased, but her eyes were watchful.

'If you must know,' he said, deciding to tell her, 'I've got my own niece there in that household. I just wondered what the husband would say about that arrangement.'

Thora almost spoilt her nice amenable manner by shouting out, 'You've *what?*' She just managed not to. She said instead, very quietly, 'Did I hear you correctly, Boyd?' And as he didn't answer but sat watching the traffic lights, waiting for them to change, she continued, 'Your own niece? But I didn't know you *had* a niece.'

'I have, and she's the bane of my life. My old friend, the professor, had her at his home, but his sister's in years and didn't want the trouble. Mrs Roberts said she didn't mind so I shifted Felicity.'

Thora couldn't get her breath back. To think that that Roberts creature was in his confidence so much and he hadn't even bothered to tell Thora herself about it. 'When was this arrangement made?' she breathed, forcing herself to be quiet.

'Oh, it was in a hurry, the last day or two. Felicity's only just arrived. I hope to heaven she won't wreck the place.'

'But Boyd, dear,' Thora protested, 'why did you approach Mrs Roberts? I mean, I've got a big home and a big family and servants who could have taken your niece in hand. Why not ask me first at least?'

'Oh, does it matter, Thora? I've so many more problems on my mind,' he said, rather impatiently, and he thought of his own home, and of what they would have done with Felicity if he had taken her there. He had never mentioned his own home to Thora and he had no intention of doing so now. 'To be honest, it slipped my mind. The child's been away at school. She's a pest. I can't think why I should have mentioned her to you, anyway. I certainly wouldn't have wanted to bother you with ideas as to what to do with her.'

'But to tell someone else – someone in my hairdresser's – all about your private problems, and not me!' She couldn't get over it.

'Good gracious, don't tell me you're hurt, Thora! I thought you'd be grateful,' he said bracingly. 'If you want to have some ideas on any subject, tell me, for heaven's sake, what I do with the brat if young Roberts turns up and is livid with his wife for taking her.'

'Oh, I doubt if he'll bother if you're paying her,' Thora said, her voice rising on a questioning note. But Boyd didn't answer that. He kept seeing Rachel's face, closed, frigid, not wanting to discuss her husband. Well, she hadn't wanted to discuss him when Boyd had put gentle questions to her, so he was quite sure Rachel was quite angry with being forced to talk about him in the hairdresser's with her boss and a customer. He kept an eye open for a parking place, near to where they were going, and he didn't bother to answer her question. Sensibly, Thora didn't press it. She would find out some other way, she promised herself.

'Well, we have a nice long time away from the hospital and problems,' she said comfortably. 'Well, we have haven't we?'

'You know I want to get back by ten, to get on with my work in the Lab,' he said, that impatience visible again.

'You mean the new way of giving anaesthetics,' she murmured, very softly, holding her breath a little and waiting for the explosion. He would hate to know the secret was out.

He glanced swiftly at her, his eyebrows raised, eyes hostile, his attention momentarily off the road. 'Look out, Boyd!' she screamed, and he flicked the wheel back, with inches to spare. 'You nearly scraped that car!'

'Then don't say things like that to me when I'm driving,' he said coldly, pulling in to the side. 'Now, where did you get that information?'

'Didn't you want me to know about your project?'

He studied her, and the coldness in his face melted a little. After all, he was treating her as a special friend. Yet somehow he hadn't wanted her to know. He had wanted to tell Rachel about it first, only that friendship hadn't ripened quickly enough, and now there was a husband, home from the sea. A little of the bitterness, the acute disappointment of that, showed in his face, as he strove to answer honestly yet tactfully. 'If you must know, I didn't want anyone to know about it, until it was perfected. How did you hear of it?' he asked again.

She shrugged. 'Your dear friend the professor might well be a clam but he has a clottish youth working with him who is bubbling over with the thrill of life in the lab and I regret I was base enough to ask *him*. I wanted to *know*, Boyd, because I think I can help you, but you don't tell me things any more. You don't confide in me.'

After a short, embarrassed silence, he said, looking away, 'If you want to know, I don't

131

tell anybody. One tends to hang on to discoveries until they can be proved.'

'Fair enough,' she agreed quietly. 'I understand that. If you really mean you haven't told anybody else, not anybody.'

'Not anybody,' he said, frigidly. 'I'm sorry you can't accept that.'

'Oh, I can, Boyd, I can. It's just that, well, I believed we were such good friends, you and I.'

He winced. He was caught in an intimate situation, a thing he always strove to avoid. Unless, of course, it was with Rachel.

He tried to bring a shutter down over his mind. He mustn't think of Rachel any more. Not his to think about. No more.

But Rachel's intense blue eyes wouldn't be banished, and he found himself wondering why she had looked so angry, so distressed, when that husband had been mentioned. Had she really thought he was dead?

'Boyd!' Thora said sharply, bringing him back. 'Aren't we? Such good friends?'

'Oh, yes, I suppose so. We'd better be getting on, I suppose.'

'And good friends help each other, and I was thinking about a man my father knows, called Ian Pepperdine.'

She watched him closely as she said it. The name arrested him from starting up the car to go again. He stared at her, and she smiled, brilliantly, pleased with her tactics.

'I thought that name might ring a bell,' she said, 'and he dines at our house. Now how would it be if my father had a word with him, and we went up to London to see him and tell him about this clever thing you've designed?'

'Ian Pepperdine,' he breathed. 'The one man who might, who just might be interested.'

Thora nodded. 'Now do you see what a lot of good I could do for you if only you'd let me, Boyd? Now don't be silly and go all upstage and say you can't accept favours. It isn't a favour. It's good sense.'

She talked to him solidly for ten minutes and in the end he had to allow that if it was taken up by this man, through the good offices of Thora's family, who had a lot of strings to pull, as Thora put it, then it would get this much-needed formula of his through in as short a time as possible. He couldn't stop the enthusiasm showing. Thora was pleased, too – at last she had managed to make an impression on him. Boyd might not want to be tempted with a private nursing home to manage, but quite clearly the things he invented were very precious to him and liable to bring in a lot of money if the right people were contacted at the right moment.

She let him drive on, then, confident that all the tiresome bits that had stuck out were all tucked neatly in. No more problems. She had swept everything away, even Rachel Roberts who, with a husband very much in evidence, wasn't likely to interest Boyd now. In fact, Thora congratulated herself, nothing was left to annoy her. She had even persuaded Lucille to go (at her expense) to Paris, for a while, and keep out of the way. Nothing, then, was left to worry her.

She had forgotten Max. Max Trent, Lucille's brother. He called at the hospital to ask to see Thora, that afternoon. It wasn't a casual visit, but one of pressing urgency. He needed more money. Thora had given him some the week before, but that had gone at the races. His dismay when he learned that Thora wasn't there, was very real.

He could usually persuade women to get information for him, especially the young ones. A young nurse racing through OP with a message, told him where he could find Dr Fenton.

That was how Rachel, sitting wondering why Hazel Otty, having had a row with Neil, should have gone running into the house again, saw a new and rather brilliantly coloured high powered low-slung car draw up outside of the salon and a very tall young man sling a leg over the outside and pull himself up to standing height. He had on a very long woollen college scarf, and a brilliant knitted jersey, but everything else was old once-expensive tweed. Rachel wondered who he could be wanting.

He came in, and leaned confidentially on her counter. 'I was told I could find Dr Fenton here. I suppose she'd be about ready to emerge from the dryer, wouldn't she?' and he smiled engagingly at Rachel.

'Oh, I'm sorry, she's gone. Another doctor called for her. They're spending the evening together.'

Max was annoyed. Thora really had good luck, the way she managed to evade him. He said, 'Do you know where they've gone?'

The Madame looked out, and Rachel explained what was going on. She said they had no idea, which wasn't very sensible since Rachel knew. But she wouldn't have told this young man in any case. There was something about him that she deeply disliked.

The Madame said, 'You'd better pack up and go, Rachel. You said you wanted to go to the dry cleaners, dear. They'll be shut if you're not careful.'

Rachel thanked her, and went to get her coat. Max still hung about. He watched her come running out. 'I say, want a lift any-where?' he called.

She shook her head, and pointed to the next door but one shop, where rows of coats hung on hangers, and the woman behind the counter was preparing to pack up for the day. A frosty dusk was setting in, creeping up the High Street like thin fog, pinkish grey in colour. For the time of year it was cold. He watched Rachel flip in, get her things, and come staggering out. She was carrying two coats and a suit, and trying to keep them off the ground in their plastic covers.

Max went over to her. 'Let me,' he said, taking them from her. 'Now, you won't refuse a lift this time, I'm quite sure!'

Rachel laughed. 'But I only live across the road. Look, in that house with the bottom lights on. In Endell Street.'

Max recovered himself. 'Then I shall carry these for you.'

'I don't really see why you should,' she objected. 'I really can manage, and you must be in a hurry – you wanted Dr Fenton.'

He looked wistful. 'If she's gone out with a man for the evening, then I shall have to find someone else to stand me the next meal,' he grinned, unrepentant.

He expected her to greet this thrust rather coldly, but oddly Rachel understood it. In Endell Street people were frank like that about their needs. Hazel's brother from next door came in unashamedly when there was nothing in the place to eat, and stood looking longingly at the meal Rachel was getting out of the oven. Thinking of Hazel's

136

brother, and certainly of Hazel who would hang around for the rest of the evening arguing with Neil, she said, 'Well, there's a big meat pie in the oven, if you'd like to stay.'

But in the end, it wasn't his hunger that made Max Trent stay for the meal, and the rest of the evening. Rachel saw to her great dismay and Neil, behind his closed eyes, sensed it. Max stayed because of Hazel.

Chapter Five

Hazel was demonstrating some dance steps. Kathy and Felicity were watching, with absorption. Hazel was very fair, and willowy. She had a sweet face, a ready smile, and eyes empty of anything beyond the world of her dancing. To dance was the one thing she wanted to do. Rachel saw with a shock that Hazel was just as empty-headed as her own mother said she was, and just as ruthless about her dancing as that shrewd person had indicated. Poor Neil, Rachel thought suddenly, with a flash of pity.

Max let Rachel introduce him and explain how it was he was here, and Neil got up impatiently and walked out of the room.

'I say, that chap, haven't I seen him before?' Max said, looking rather shocked.

Kathy, oddly enough, leapt to Neil's defence. 'Well, he doesn't look that awful, does he? He's only blind, through an accident, and it doesn't show, and he's marvellous at getting about doing things, and he types all his own work and he doesn't have any mistakes, not like some people I know who can't type a single letter without scrubbing out.'

Rachel bit her lip in compunction. It was

all very well Kathy leaping to Neil's defence like that, but did she have to shout? He must have heard every word. And while she was thinking that, it struck her that Max wasn't shocked at the figure Neil presented since his accident, but at something else that she didn't know about, and which seemed to her to be merely recognition; someone Max had known, or seen and remembered, from the days before the accident. 'He's a journalist,' she said slowly, wondering if that was the connection.

Max didn't stay after supper. Hazel was leaving, having had words again with Neil. Rachel was glad she was going. Glad, too, that Max wasn't staying any longer. There was this important discussion about Charlie Roberts, and so little time to embark on it, Rachel fretted.

At the door, Max said, 'Thanks for the meal. Sorry I scrounged it. I do, sometimes. I'll send you some flowers tomorrow.' With the money he would pick up from Dr Fenton, he promised himself.

Hazel was waiting at her gate, pretending to untie a knot in her shoe. Rachel shut her door, and Max stood looking at Hazel.

'If you were a gentleman, you'd help me,' Hazel sniffed.

'If I were a gentleman, young Hazel, I wouldn't snaffle you from that poor blind bloke in there, which I fully intend to do. See that car parked outside the hairdressers?'

'Yes, it's yours, isn't it?' Hazel said. 'I heard Rachel telling Neil how you came to pick her up. Do you really want to see Dr Fenton?'

'Never you mind,' he murmured. 'I expect you'd like a trial run, to see if you like my car, wouldn't you?'

He walked her to the top of the road, her coat slung round her slender shoulders. 'How far will you go to achieve a dancing career?' he asked her.

'Never you mind about my career,' she said darkly. 'I'm taking care of that. You just tell me about yourself and how it is you're not out with some other girl yourself.'

Ruthless, he thought. She honestly wants to be a dancer.

Kathy watched them, from the landing window. Rachel, behind her, said in a low tone, full of meaning. 'If you say one word to Neil about that, you'll have to account to me!'

Kathy said smartly, 'Do you think he doesn't know? If he doesn't, Felicity will tell him, anyway. Why? Because she likes stirring things up – she said so!'

In the end, Rachel didn't talk to Neil about it until the two younger girls were settled with Deirdre and Mrs Pym in front of television. 'Neil, you can't think what happened today,' she said, and she repeated as nearly as possible what had occurred at

140

the hairdresser's. 'She was so sure. Who is this man whose name is Charlie Roberts, that she's found?'

Neil said, 'Tell me it all over again, slowly. Let me think.'

Rachel did. Neil said, 'You wouldn't have minded very much if Boyd Ingram hadn't been there, would you?'

'Why do you say that?' she whispered.

'I never used to believe it when I heard that people who lost their sight had their other senses become sharpened,' Neil said, 'but it's true. I can hear more tones under-lying people's words than I ever did before.'

'And you think I'm silly enough to have fallen for Boyd Ingram?' she demanded, but to her disgust, her tones weren't angry, and her voice shook. 'Well, it won't get me anywhere. No, Neil, let's be sensible. Who could it be? Or did she just find out, and pretended she'd met someone?'

'There *is* a Charlie Roberts in your life,' Neil said slowly, 'so it follows that somehow she met him and put two and two together. I don't think Charlie would have the wit to do so himself, do you?'

'*Kathy's brother?* Oh, no!' Rachel whispered, horrified.

'Well, let's not go all to pieces,' Neil said coolly. 'If this Dr Ingram does mean any-thing to you, then I suggest you tell him everything.'

'But Neil, when I wanted to, you advised me not to. You said you wouldn't like the plan, if you were the fellow.'

'I know I did,' Neil agreed, 'but that was before this happened. It's a little different now, isn't it? As I see it, this Dr Fenton wants Dr Ingram. Why? Is he wealthy?'

Rachel sat down slowly and thought about it. 'I don't believe so. She's always trying to persuade him to go to a smart practice in London, I've heard people say. I've actually heard her gently persuading him to wear something smarter only he doesn't like that. Not for every day. He wears old casual things. But when he calls for her, he looks terribly well dressed and ... uncomfortable in them.'

'It fits,' Neil said wearily. 'Well, you can do no harm in trying to tell him. The only thing is, if he really wants her, he may tell her and she'll tell Madame and you'll lose your job. Do you mind?'

'Yes, of course I do. That was the whole point of the thing,' Rachel said angrily. 'Oh, I suppose I could get something else, but not with all those bonuses. I don't know why Madame is so generous, mind. I'm quite sure I'm not worth all that to her, even if I don't mind what hours I work, but just the same, it's a useful position and I don't like the thought of that awful Dr Fenton being the one to lose me that job.'

'I can't think of anything else,' Neil said quietly. 'And now, having tried my best to do something for you, will you do something for me? Tell me if Hazel went out with that Trent fellow.'

Rachel's silence was enough. She just couldn't bring herself to say no, or that she didn't know. All she said was, 'Oh, Neil!'

'I had it coming to me, I suppose,' he said, at last. 'And I could hear how she talked to him, all through supper. I'm not a fool.'

'Oh, Neil!' Rachel said again, helplessly, because Hazel would be no use to him. They all knew that – even if he weren't blind, she'd be no use to him. She loathed his work, except where it could help hers.

'I just wish I could remember where I've met him before, that's all,' Neil said angrily. 'I know his voice. Describe him to me again.' So Rachel did, but it really didn't help. They had to let it go.

There were other problems, anyway. Kathy and Felicity didn't get on, and Neil sent them out most of the day. To walk, to go shopping – anything, so that he could think.

Mrs Pym said, 'You didn't ought to do that, my dear,' which made Neil writhe. 'After all, we all know what happens to young girls who are such flibberty-jibbets as those two, and what would Dr Ingram say if anything should happen to that young niece

143

of his?'

'Probably he'd say it served her right, and the person who did it to her,' Neil said unfeelingly. But he took it back at once. As Mrs Pym said, 'We all think it's someone else's girl whose going to get hurt, but it has to be someone's, and suppose it *was* to be Dr Ingram's niece, or Kathy?'

Thora pursued this profitable line with Boyd Ingram, too. 'I wish you hadn't left your niece with those Arden people. There's something not quite right in that household, from what you've told me. Shall I go and see them, unexpectedly, and see for myself how Felicity is getting on?' but Boyd would never countenance this.

'Leave well alone, Thora,' was his invariable response.

'Still, I wish you'd take her away, and let me take her to my home. She wouldn't be any trouble there,' Thora urged.

It was Rachel's day for going to the shop in the morning. Boyd and Thora descended on them after lunch. Everyone was in the kitchen, and there was a hot overpowering smell which Thora couldn't at first place, and which she found sickening and said so, loudly.

At the sound of her voice at the open door at which they had arrived, all laughter and loud conversation snapped off suddenly and everyone looked in that direction. Neil said,

'Who is it there, Rachel?'

Rachel didn't answer at first. Her eyes were locked with Boyd's, in an unswerving gaze neither could tear apart, and the wide happy smile had frozen on her face. Felicity said, 'Oh, it's my Uncle Boyd, come the back way to catch me out in something. Well, we're only making toffee apples. See what you can make of that!' she said rudely.

Dr Fenton's face suffused with colour, partly with embarrassment because she was so sure she wouldn't find any such happy family occupation proceeding, and partly with indignation to think that a thirteen-year-old could be so rude to Boyd.

'You've no right to speak like that to your uncle – apologize at once!' she stormed at Felicity.

Mrs Pym looked as if she were going to cry. Boyd and Rachel managed to stop looking at each other, Rachel because she turned away to speak to Felicity. 'Spoiling things, isn't it?' she murmured. Dr Fenton couldn't hear what she said, but Felicity reddened. 'Well,' she said, grumbling, 'I don't know her and she doesn't know me. Why should she talk to me like that?'

Rachel said, 'Quite, so show her you know good manners by apologizing – it'll be a score up to you,' so Felicity said fiercely to Boyd, 'Sorry – shouldn't have said that, but I thought it just the same.'

'And you'd be right, I fear,' Boyd sighed. 'You see, Thora, there is nothing untoward going on. And we've spoilt the fun. Rachel, may I have a word with you before we go?' and as she nodded, he turned to Neil. 'How are you, old chap?' and Neil said sarcastically that he felt fine, as someone who was looking for Dr Fenton had made off with his girl-friend and upset everything. 'He said his name was Max Trent,' Neil added for good measure.

Dr Fenton drew a sharp breath. 'When was this? What did he want?' she demanded.

Boyd didn't wait to hear the answer to that. He filtered into the room, tasted the toffee that was being dropped all over the apples, and asked Mrs Pym how she did. He grinned comfortably at Deirdre and asked Kathy if she'd mind if he had an apple before it set.

Dr Fenton noticed, while she questioned Neil about Max, that Boyd moved about the kitchen with comfort and ease. Kittens were running up the back of his jacket. He turfed the big cat out of the rocker and sat in it, and the cat retaliated by jumping up on to his lap and kneading his trousers until the surface was roughened. 'Boyd, don't let that wretched creature do that!' Thora Fenton said sharply, but he only grinned and tickled the cat under its chin and rolled up a screw of paper into a ball for the kittens to play with. Everyone talked at once, and the hubbub seemed right and natural in this comfortable kitchen.

Rachel was making tea at the stove. She gave a cup to Boyd without asking him if he wanted it. Thora Fenton saw with indignation that Rachel knew he took three teaspoonsful of sugar. She watched, and saw them exchange that searching look, a look that needed no words. It took her breath away that anyone like Rachel should be able to command from Boyd such an easy happy comfortable manner, when she herself had to work so hard on him. Presently, after scarcely tasting the tea she had been given, Thora got up and said, 'Boyd, we ought to go.'

He got up, and Rachel picked the kittens off him and dropped them into Deirdre's lap. He said goodbye to everyone and went out to the car with Thora Fenton. But once out there, he suddenly came back, as if he had forgotten something. Rachel, at the back door with a jelly in her hands to put in the outside safe to set, looked up in surprise. 'I thought you'd forgotten,' she said.

He smiled. 'I wanted to apologize for this intrusion, that's all. I could hardly do it in front of Dr Fenton and the others.'

'Well, I have something special I wanted to say to you,' Rachel burst out. 'I would have liked more time to explain, it's about Charlie Roberts.'

'Oh, no, leave that alone,' Boyd said hastily. 'Don't let's talk about him. What I wanted to say, too, was that I'll still drive you to the Library to do your cousin's research unless your husband can do that.'

'Boyd, there isn't a husband,' she said desperately.

He stared. 'You mean there's no such person as Charlie Roberts?' he said slowly.

She reddened. 'Oh, yes, there is such a person and–'

'Then there *is* a husband. I take it he could be nothing else?' he said stiffly, angrily.

'Oh, it's so difficult to explain,' she said, and then Thora Fenton came briskly towards them.

'Goodness, I thought you said you would only be a minute, Boyd,' she smiled. 'Really, Mrs Roberts, if you knew how poor Dr Ingram is rushed off his feet at the hospital, I'm sure you wouldn't keep him talking about that sister of yours. At least, I suppose you were discussing Deirdre? I know you're worried about her, but she *is* my patient,' so there the matter rested. Rachel had only made matters worse by trying to explain.

A curious new set of circumstances arose out of that unexpected visit of Boyd and Dr Fenton, however; Rachel didn't realize what was happening at first, but like Boyd, Dr Fenton took to dropping in whenever she happened to be down that end of the

High Street.

Rachel couldn't believe it at first. She heard about it from Felicity who didn't like her. 'Why didn't you say that horrible woman comes here?' she demanded of Rachel. 'That Dr Fenton who's after Uncle Boyd?'

'What are you talking about?' Rachel asked, mystified. She was helping Felicity to make her bed, which was awkwardly placed, right up in the corner, and a great temptation for a thirteen-year-old not to make the effort but to fling the cover over in the day-time.

'Well, that day we were making toffee apples, it seemed as if she'd never been before, but she must have, because she just comes in as if she lives here.'

'She does *what?*' Rachel gasped.

'Well, she dropped in one day with a bundle of magazines for Deirdre,' Felicity said, rather unwillingly. 'Plushy ones. Deirdre said after she'd gone that she never had mags like that.'

'So that's where they came from,' Rachel frowned. 'But why wouldn't Deirdre tell me? She always does.'

Felicity looked sly. 'Perhaps she thought you'd send them back. Maybe that's why Neil didn't happen to mention that That Woman was here to tea with him. Sitting talking to him about someone she knows who runs a technical paper and wants special articles, so she *said*.'

'When was this? Felicity, are you making it up?' Rachel said fiercely.

'Please yourself, but I thought you'd like to know and if you don't want to, I can easy dry up,' Felicity snapped with a fine disregard for her grammar.

'Don't be silly,' Rachel begged, cross with herself for losing ground with the child, when she did seem to be getting somewhere at last. 'Come and help me make Kathy's bed.'

'No, we're not supposed to go in her room. I'll help you make Neil's and Deirdre's if you like,' Felicity said quickly.

'Where *is* Kathy, by the way?' Rachel asked suddenly.

'Gone to one of her school friend's houses, I believe,' Felicity said airily. 'Of course, if you've been to boarding school like me, you don't behave in that childish way, popping round to other people's houses to play.'

Rachel hid a smile, and talked to Felicity about the thing she seemed to like doing best: playing the instruments she had brought with her.

Felicity sniffed. 'That old Neil never lets me play, and he can't be thinking about his work *all* the time, so I shall just have to find someone else who would like to hear some music. Maybe the Ottys. I bet Hazel Otty's mother would be thrilled to hear my

Spanish serenade.'

Rachel was very worried about these disclosures. She tackled Neil first about a time and a place for Felicity to play her instruments. 'I don't want to worry you, Neil, but we *are* getting paid for the child to be here, and some part of the day she ought to be allowed to practise.'

'Who's stopping her?' Neil said, in an odd voice.

'I don't know, my dear, but I did gather that you want to be quiet to work–'

'Is this another of your special arguments?' Neil said, in an unfriendly voice, totally unlike him.

'Neil! What's the matter, my dear? Are you in pain?' Rachel cried, completely mystified. 'Well, you don't talk to *me* like that, my dear, so what is it?'

He sat woodenly. She went and sat down beside him and tried to take his hand but he snatched it away.

'All right, so you want the ward of your dear doctor friend to have freedom to make a ghastly noise on her musical instruments. Very well. It's your house!'

'But Neil, dear, only for say half an hour a day! Felicity says you never let her have a chance to practise at all!'

'And you believe her, of course!'

'No, not necessarily. I don't necessarily care about Felicity's music time, either,

151

Neil,' Rachel said slowly. 'What I do care about is your manner to me. If something's wrong, my dear, do for heaven's sake be frank and *tell* me!'

His face was white, she noticed, and his mouth set in a tight line. He sat silent, but at last, goaded by something she didn't understand, he said, 'Very well. If you must "have it out", as I believe it is called, I just hope you're glad you've got your own way about Hazel, that's all!'

'My own way about Hazel?' she repeated, mystified. 'Neil, dear, what *is* all this about? All right, that Max Trent did go off with her, but he didn't abduct her. She went willingly, or so it appeared to me.'

'You were watching?'

'I happened to glance out of the landing window – to see what was interesting Kathy, if you must know.'

'But it was your manoeuvring that made Hazel take off from me,' he accused in a low voice. 'Oh, you can't say Dr Fenton was wrong about that, no matter how much you dislike her. Don't forget I happen to know only too well that you never thought Hazel was good enough for me.'

Rachel looked deeply hurt. 'That may well be true, Neil,' she said steadily, 'but so far as I know, I've never done a thing to let her think I feel like that, and I certainly wasn't responsible for her drifting away from you

152

nor the rows you two had. Don't blame me for that, *please*, Neil!'

As he didn't answer, Rachel went on, in a low passionate voice, 'I don't know why that Dr Fenton is doing this, why she's bothering to do it, but I can see she's making mischief in this house. It *was* her who made you think I'd turned Hazel away, wasn't it?'

'Don't be silly, Rachel! It doesn't need a stranger to force me to see anything! I've got ears, haven't I? I've heard you say a thousand times, that Hazel wasn't good enough for me. I suppose that means that she isn't good enough to be related to you by marriage. It doesn't need anyone to tell me, either, how persuasive you can be, whether you want someone to come, or someone to go. You wanted Hazel to go.'

'Neil, that isn't true,' Rachel cried, deeply distressed. 'And if you'll think that of me, *me*, your *friend*, then you'll think anything! But it *is* that Dr Fenton. I can see it now. She's bringing Deirdre plushy magazines that we can't afford. Not so long ago Deirdre couldn't bear the sound of her name, but I notice that's all stopped now. And Dr Fenton will interfere between Kathy and me, too, if I don't watch things. But what can I do? I'm away from the house so much.'

'You just don't like Dr Fenton. You're jealous of her, because of her having a

153

friendship with Dr Ingram, aren't you?' Neil thrust, with accuracy.

'No, not jealous, Neil, dear. Just hoist on my own petard. That's another thing. I tried to tell Boyd Ingram the truth about that matter, but *she* came back to find him. She won't leave him alone!'

Neil had no answer about that. He was sitting thinking about Hazel and hating everything because she had gone off with a man who not only had his sight, but a low-slung high-powered car.

Rachel got up. 'Well, if you're determined to think I'm to blame about Hazel, the only thing to do is for me to try to get her back.'

'No!' Neil thundered the word, swivelling round in his chair to stare in the direction of Rachel's voice. 'Do you think I've got no pride – no self-respect. I know she's gone on her own two feet and won't come back and I don't want any begging. What I can't take is the thought that you've niggled and niggled at her until she did go.'

'Neil, that isn't *true!*' Rachel burst out. 'Oh, Neil, don't let's quarrel. We've got to keep together, you and me, for Deirdre's sake, and for Kathy's. I've tried to hold this family together, and it worked, until that Dr Fenton found us. What have we done to her that she should single us out to make things unhappy for us?'

'It's not just that. It's a matter of some

MSS I sent off,' Neil said, in a stifled voice. 'You said you'd post them for me ... last Tuesday. They never got there, and if they do now, it will be too late for them to be used. They happened to be topical articles. You may not have realized but that was why I asked you to take them to the Post Office. At my speed I wouldn't have got there in time.'

'I know it, Neil. I realize their importance. How do you know they didn't get there in time?'

'Because my editor has sent them back with the outer envelopes to show the date mark on them. That is proof. If you didn't want to be bothered, why didn't you say and I'd have asked a neighbour to do it?'

'It wasn't a case of not wanting to do it,' Rachel said urgently. 'I took them and willing but the Madame wouldn't let me go out to the Post Office, so sooner than lose the post, I asked one of the other girls to post them. She was going out. And I can trust her!'

'It looks like it. Fancy giving them to a stranger, and you only a few doors away from the Post Office.'

'Oh, Neil, the length of the High Street is between us and I did so much want them to get there in time.'

He got them out of the table drawer and threw them across to her. 'If you doubt me, read what my editor says. Good work, acceptable, but arrived too late. And look at the date stamps.'

He was right. Rachel couldn't understand it. She said wrathfully, 'Bunty took them with her. I'll telephone her to find out what happened.'

'Don't bother. It's all of a piece with your treatment of Hazel,' Neil said bitterly.

'Now look, Neil, I can understand you thinking I pushed Hazel out of your life, but why should I destroy the other lucrative medium – apart from my own – coming into this house? I depend on your income as much as what I earn, so that wouldn't be sense, now, would it?'

She left him thinking that over, and went to telephone Bunty. Bunty, however, said at once that she hadn't taken the letters to the Post Office because she had run into Kathy, who offered to. Bunty thought it was all right, and didn't even bother to mention it when she returned.

Now Neil would be very angry, Rachel thought. Her own annoyance towards Kathy arose when Kathy came storming into the house with Felicity. 'Kathy, did you post Neil's letters to his editor last Tuesday?'

Kathy skidded to a halt and her face slowly reddened. 'What if I did?' she demanded.

Her confusion told the exasperated Rachel all she wanted to know. Kathy must have forgotten, and posted them much later and decided to say nothing. She glared defiantly at Rachel, who said, shrugging, 'Neil's had them returned. They were good and would have sold but they got there too late.'

'Not through me,' Kathy said, sticking her chin out. 'I did post them at once, I did, I did, and you can't say I didn't. Dr Fenton's right – you blame all of us no matter how much we try to help you.'

Dr Fenton again. Rachel closely questioned Kathy about it, but got nowhere. Kathy dried up and refused to say another word about it. The thing was getting too big for Rachel. She went to find Deirdre.

Deirdre was in the sitting-room talking quietly to Neil. She had been saying, '…and she's always been so good to us but Dr Fenton said that Rachel…'

'Just what did Dr Fenton say about Rachel?' Rachel demanded from the open door. 'All right, Deirdre, I did hear but I wasn't listening purposely. I came back to speak to Neil.'

Deirdre looked fussed. 'There you are, you see,' she muttered. 'Well, it's no use looking at me like that, Rachel. You *did* hear just now and Dr Fenton warned us that you'd listen in to our conversations and do all sorts of things to make things difficult for us.'

'What's the matter with everybody?' Rachel burst out. 'Neil, you used to be so shrewd at assessing people's characters. And you, Deirdre, not so long ago, there wasn't a good word you could say about Dr Fenton.'

'Well, she's certainly being nice to me now, and you're not.' Deirdre's voice shook a little but she was determined. 'You're just not as nice as you used to be, Rachel, or you wouldn't have taken all those magazines away from me. You know how much they meant to me – I can't afford to buy glossies like those.'

'What are you talking about? I haven't *seen* the magazines!'

'Well, it's a funny thing to me that they've vanished. Kathy and Felicity wouldn't take them, neither would Mrs Pym or Neil, so that only leaves you!' Deirdre said, and wheeled herself swiftly out of the room. Neil got up to feel his way out, too. Rachel said sharply, 'Oh, sit down, Neil, and I'll go. I have things to do, anyway.'

Tears stung her eyes. Never had this family been so driven apart as now. Mrs Pym followed her into the kitchen and dumped down her cleaning rags and looked thoughtfully at Rachel.

Rachel said, 'Well, are *you* going to range yourself on the side of the enemy?'

Mrs Pym said hardily, 'I don't know what you mean, dear. But if it's anything to you, I just heard all of that, and I could have told you it would happen, that day *she* came in with Dr Ingram. The minute I caught sight of him looking at you that funny way, and her seeing it, I thought to myself, ah, now, the fat will be in the fire for sure.'

Rachel wiped her eyes. 'What funny way did he look at me? As I remember it, he was annoyed because of … well, something he'd heard.'

'That you was married,' Mrs Pym said. 'And in case you want to say something about that, yes, well, I *did* listen at the doors. I always do if I like people and want to know what's going on. Well, if you ask me, you don't look like a young married woman, and that's a fact. And what is more, you forgot your neighbours know you're not married.'

Rachel's hand flew to her mouth.

Mrs Pym laughed. 'Oh, not to worry. They're nice neighbours. They wouldn't tell anyone, though I must say I don't think much of a tale like you pitched, just to get that job. What's so special about the job, eh?'

'Shut the door, so Deirdre won't hear,' Rachel said distractedly. 'I don't know what's gone wrong. I've been there for months and nothing was said. Now all of a sudden, Dr Fenton appears at the hairdressers (the last thing I expected, for her to go to a small shop like that!) and everything's gone to pieces. It wasn't a bad thing to do. It was just that that job was going to suit me so well, and I happened to know you had to be married, to get it – because of Mrs York's flighty husband, you see. Well, why are you pulling that face? Housekeepers and cooks used to call themselves "Mrs", didn't they?'

'Yes, but it was known whether they were married or not,' Mrs Pym said, thinking. 'What was so special about *that* job, may I ask?'

'I can see this house from where I sit. It matters. Don't tell Deirdre I told you, but one day when she was here by herself, she opened the door to a knock and the man seemed to be the repair man we'd been expecting, only he wasn't, and he would have attacked her, only a neighbour was coming in at the back, and the man got away. Deirdre's never been the same since. Being in a wheelchair, you see, made her feel so helpless.'

'Oh, the beast!' Mrs Pym said wrathfully. 'Well, now I'm here, you don't have to worry, do you? Why don't you get another job and drop this business of pretending there's a husband?'

'It's too late,' Rachel said dully. 'Dr Fenton's found my husband, you see.'

'Now what does that mean? You just said there wasn't one.'

'I know. But there it is. The other day, in the hairdressers, she said he'd come to the hospital and was a patient of hers, with a rash he'd picked up at sea. Well, my boss was there, so I couldn't say there isn't such a person as Charlie Roberts, could I? And one lie led to another, because Dr Fenton kept asking questions.'

'She would! If there's one person I can't stand, dear, it's that woman!'

'Thank goodness there's one of you on my side,' Rachel said. 'Unfortunately I hadn't briefed Dr Ingram and he believed what I told Dr Fenton and when I tried to tell him afterwards, he wouldn't listen.'

'Oh, now the fat's in the fire!' Mrs Pym said. 'That's a great pity, I must say. And what's all this business of you and your cousin?' She put her things away in the cupboard as she spoke. 'If there's one thing I liked, the minute I come here, it was the way you and that Neil got on together. What made him go on like he did today?'

'I wonder you didn't hear that much,' Rachel couldn't help saying. Mrs Pym might well be harmless and acting in her interests, but it wasn't nice to think she listened at the door.

'I would have done,' Mrs Pym said, unashamed, 'only I got there too late. The row was half over. I thought it might be about that fancy little baggage next door, Hazel Otty.'

'It *was* about her. Neil thinks I was responsible for her going away, and that I'd never liked her.'

'Well, you know who put *that* into his head,' Mrs Pym said. 'It's not my place to say anything, but I'd have liked to keep that Dr Fenton from coming in. She drops in any time, and she's setting them all against you, dear. I could give her a piece of my mind, that I could!'

'I thought that might be the case,' Rachel choked. 'Well, it's gone too far now.'

'No, it's not! You just get along to Dr Ingram and make him listen to the truth, that you're not married. That's the first thing to do.'

'He wouldn't listen, I told you so. Besides, what makes you think it would interest him, Mrs Pym? He's going to marry Dr Fenton. Anyone can see that with half an eye. They're both doctors, and she wants it, and she's his kind. So don't argue.'

'Well, that's as maybe, but I would like to know where she found this fella she says admits to being your husband, dear. That's a thing that ought to be put a stop to, whether it's because of Dr Ingram or not. All sorts of mischief can lead out of it.'

The mischief, indeed, began the next day. Rachel was with Neil, again trying to persuade him that he was thinking wrong things about her, when the doorbell rang.

Irritably, because she thought it was Kathy or Felicity playing about, Rachel called out,

'Open it – it isn't locked!'

It opened and closed quietly enough. Rachel and Neil took no notice. Their own argument was real, perhaps more real because they so rarely argued. The opening of the door to the room they were in, made Neil stop and listen. His ears were the keenest to pick up the sound of strange footsteps.

'Who is it?' he demanded of Rachel.

'What are you doing here?' he heard Rachel say on a low angry note.

'Now there's a thing to say to your own loving husband,' a man's voice said laughingly.

'I know that voice,' Neil said. 'What's he doing here? You said he'd gone to sea, Rachel.'

'Well, and so I did,' Charlie Roberts laughed. 'But it was a voyage of short duration on account of me not getting on with the ship's cook, so I jumped the boat at Marseilles and thought I'd hitch a lift overland (which I did) and come back to my dear sister Kathy, oh, and not forgetting my loving wife.'

Chapter Six

There was stunned silence in the room. Unwittingly Neil and Rachel drew together, their quarrel forgotten, in this new hazard. Neil said again, 'What's he doing here?' and on consideration, 'Where's Kathy?'

'Out,' Rachel said shortly. And to Charlie Roberts, she said, 'Where did you get that officer's uniform?'

'Oh, now that is another story. A little matter of borrowing it, as you might say, from my stable companion, when I fell into the water and got soaked, it being so cold and me not having the means to dry my things. Whatever else you can accuse poor old Charlie Roberts of, it is not of being helpless. He's a likely lad for looking after himself.'

'Don't we know it?' Neil said bitterly. 'Well, it's no use coming scrounging here. We're about as hard up as we ever were.'

'Now, that is not nice, is it, Rachel, love?' Charlie said. But he didn't attempt to come near her. He leaned over the back of a chair and looked consideringly round the room.

'Get out,' Neil said on a low bitter note, but Charlie laughed.

'I'm not doing a thing, and anyway, who are you going to call to put me out?'

It broke Rachel's heart to see the way Neil whitened. Before the accident, he would have put Charlie (big as he was) out on to the pavement, in no time. Neil had studied Judo for pleasure, and because he had always averred that a newspaperman shouldn't be without that knowledge, the places he had to go into. But now it was different. Helplessly he sat at the table, knowing that even if he got up to try and do something, Charlie would lead him all over the place, and he would wreck it but not be able to touch the other man. Sound alone was now no use to him.

Rachel said, 'Just what is this, Charlie? You can't see Kathy. You agreed to that, when we had her here.'

'Oh, as to that, who wants to see Kathy?' Charlie said easily. He was a handsome man, with hair that curled tightly where Kathy's was dead straight; eyes that twinkled with laughter, malicious laughter, where Kathy's were sombre, and a mouth that turned up in a most taking way where his sister's was sullen. They were alike in colouring and the shape of features, but their natures were far apart.

Rachel saw all this in despair as she looked at him. She said, 'How – what made you come here and say I was your wife?'

'Ah, what you mean is, how did I know you were shamelessly using my name and pretending to be my wife? Now that's a bad thing for a young woman to do.'

'It wasn't bad. And there was no reason why you should know about it. It was only the Roberts bit, and it was a family name,' Rachel snapped.

'Ah, then, Dr Fenton, nice lady that she is, must have been the one telling the lies, wouldn't you say? For she said to me, Roberts, Charlie Roberts? Well, that's a coincidence. Would you be related to Rachel Roberts who lives in Endell Street? Mrs Charles Roberts, she calls herself.'

Neil let out a long breath. Rachel thought, amazedly, that she had Dr Fenton to thank, at least, for bringing herself and Neil together again. For he now quite clearly saw the hand of mischief where it was – at Dr Fenton's door.

Charlie said, in a pleased way, 'Well, I wasn't the one to say it was no such thing and that Rachel was telling lies, so I kidded her along and what do I hear but this Mrs Charlie Roberts is working at the hairdressers and doing very nicely, with bonuses and such? Well, here I am at my beam ends, so I thought I could at least come and live in my wife's house for a bit, until I get another ship, shall we say?'

Rachel looked at Neil. If only she could

catch his attention, make him give her a lead what to do. She asked herself again, did she really need that job? Why not tell them she had pretended to be married, or just leave, anyway? But there were those bonuses, that helped the family so much.

'What do you want? You can't stay here and you know it,' she said, and at that moment she saw Boyd's car draw up, and Boyd get out and stand talking to Hazel Otty on the pavement outside. 'Oh, no,' she whispered. 'It's Boyd.'

Neil heard, and didn't move. Unfortunately Charlie Roberts also heard. 'Oh, well now, that alters the situation, doesn't it?' he murmured. 'For that is the man that that nice lady Dr Fenton is wanting to marry. Now, I will have to tell her that he visits here, won't I, if I don't get some help? Mind, I wouldn't want to give you away, Rachel.'

'He's only come here to see his niece,' Rachel said sharply, but the next moment she realized she had played into Charlie's hands.

'Well, if that's all, then I'll stay, and you can introduce your loving husband to him.'

Neil said, 'If you want money, you'd better make yourself scarce till Dr Ingram has gone. That's a condition, Charlie,' and as always, when Charlie saw that Neil meant business, he complied. He went quietly out of the back way as Dr Ingram came in at the front.

Neil said quietly, listening to the approaching footsteps, 'We shall have to give him money to keep away, until we think this one out, Rachel. We can't do much in a hurry.'

She agreed, but she hadn't the time to compose her face before Boyd Ingram came in. He looked at them both and said sharply, 'What's wrong?'

Neil thought, puzzled, that for a man who was thinking of marrying another doctor, he was singularly perspicacious regarding Rachel. But like Rachel, he found the time too short to think that one out, before he could answer Boyd Ingram. 'A bit of an argument. All my fault,' Neil said, and Rachel said, backing him up, 'No, my fault entirely, but it's all right again now. Isn't it, Neil?' and that last bit was important. She hung on to Neil's reply, and when he said, 'Yes, all right now, Rachel,' she visibly relaxed, and Boyd, watching her, wondered whether she was keen on that cousin, in spite of the husband who was purported to be so handsome.

He said, 'I'd like to see Felicity about something, Rachel, and you come, too, will you? Nothing to interest you here, Neil, old chap. Purely domestic, I'm afraid,' and he took Rachel out of the room.

'Felicity's out, I think,' she began.

'I know. Hazel's just told me where Felicity is. In a shop in the High Street, buying impossible make-up which includes false eye-lashes.'

'Oh, Boyd, I'm sorry, but I didn't know. I should have kept a better watch on her.' She sounded worried, too anxious for the problem, he thought. He looked more closely at her. She looked tired, too.

'I blame myself for asking you to have her. You've got enough worries on your shoulders. But to be honest, I don't know where to take her. Dr Fenton wanted her in her own home, but I hardly think–'

Rachel's head shot up. 'Did she? Why? Oh, I shouldn't have said that, I suppose. You're close friends, you and Dr Fenton, so naturally she'd expect to have your ward with her.'

'Well, I'd rather Felicity was with you, if you can stand it,' he said. 'That is, if your husband doesn't mind, Rachel.'

'Oh, Boyd, let's have this nonsense over with,' Rachel exploded. 'There isn't a husband!'

'That is what Kathy said, when I first came here. I thought it meant that he was dead. I've looked on you as a widow. But there it is, Dr Fenton met him–'

'Boyd, he does exist, someone called Charlie Roberts, but I am not married to him,' she said heatedly. 'He's Kathy's brother and–'

Boyd lifted her left hand. She usually took the wedding ring off when she came home but this time she had forgotten. She remembered belatedly what Deirdre had said once, that it was unlucky to wear a wedding ring and to keep taking it off, when you were single. Rachel, who wasn't superstitious, and had many reasons for liking to work in that particular place, had been impatient. But now things weren't working out at all.

'Then who is your husband, because I'm quite sure you wouldn't wear this ring if you weren't married to someone,' he said earnestly. 'Is it a way of telling me to mind my own business?'

She looked wildly at him. She might have known that to someone like Boyd, it was just as bad to pretend to be married as to tell lies and any of the other things he had said he considered reprehensible.

She drew a deep breath and decided to take him in to Neil and let Neil do the explaining. But Boyd forestalled her.

'I'm sorry, my dear, I shouldn't put you to this distress. It really is no concern of mine what your circumstances are. Only to someone like me, times are not much different for unprotected women than they ever were. There's a lot of talk about women being equal, but sometimes I think about you and the burden you carry here with Neil and Deirdre, to say nothing of young Kathy, and I – well, I worry about you. All right, it's none of my business and I will stop it on the instant. That is a promise.'

She felt so choked she couldn't answer. The one thing in the world that she would have liked to know was that Boyd Ingram worried about her.

He said briskly, 'Now, let us talk about Felicity. Is she doing anything else that I should know about? Where is she getting the money to squander? You're not giving her any, are you?'

She shook her head, and endeavoured to listen to what he was saying about the amount Felicity was allowed (which seemed far too much) and about the clothes he would like Rachel to go out and buy for her, leaving it to Rachel's taste and good sense. He was now the guardian, thinking of what was best for a girl of thirteen who behaved like seventeen and was likely to go on behaving like that. The thought of someone who said she was married to an attractive young naval officer, was thrust to the back of his mind. And why not, Rachel asked herself? It was Dr Fenton who came first. She was the one he always quoted. Her name tripped so quickly and easily off his tongue. Rachel forced herself to concentrate and finally to say a composed goodbye to him when he went off again.

The problem of Charlie Roberts was still there, however. She went back to Neil, to hear what he had to say about it.

They talked about it for over an hour. 'He's a bad man,' Neil said at last. 'We mustn't give him the chance to take root in this house. We fought against it in the past and we've got to fight again.'

'Neil, I know. But in the past it was enough to warn him that we'd report some of the things we knew he was doing, if he didn't go away and leave us alone, and that appeared to be enough. But it isn't any more. He's confident now, and do you know what I think? I think Dr Fenton's putting this into his head. I know it doesn't sound probable, but I believe it is. He was … cocky almost. He'll be back for money.'

'Then we must give it to him for the time being, until we can think.' Neil held his head briefly in his hands. 'Oh, if only I weren't blind. You need someone to look after you, Rachel, and I'm no good. I'm just a burden. No, I'm not being sorry for myself. I know it. Only most days I can forget, comforting myself that I'm doing a useful enough job to earn something. But I confess that those last rejections were a jolt.'

'I'll post them personally next time, Neil,' she promised urgently.

He smiled thinly. 'No, my dear, I'll get the

172

work done sooner and go all the way myself. You've got enough on your mind. But that's not all. It's this ... this business of Kathy's brother. Before the accident, I could handle him, or anybody else. But now ... well, it's just a new worry, a new hazard I can't cope with.'

Neil decided at last that they just had to give up the bonus money, if Charlie demanded as much as that.

'But Neil, we can't. It's weak! He'll be back for more, and more, and more. You know what he's like. Goodness knows where he'll stop. Oh, if only I'd never said I was married. I applied for that job and when she said no, only married women employed here, I ... I lost my head. I can hear myself saying now, "That's right and I'm married".'

Neil said nothing. It was done, and at the time it had seemed all right. They had no compensation for the accident. They had all been a little scared as to whether they would be able to manage. Rachel's own job had folded up because of the time she had had to take off, going to the hospital, and running the house without help. It had shaken their lives up, and Neil had been as content with the new arrangement as any of the others. He couldn't blame Rachel. But now it was recoiling on them in some queer way that he didn't understand and it seemed to tie up with Dr Fenton.

He sat frowning, and Rachel couldn't reach him, so lost in his thoughts was he. They were again jolted out of their conversation by the telephone ringing.

Rachel went to answer it and was surprised to find Kathy flinging herself down the stairs. She tried to snatch the receiver from Rachel, who held it from her. 'It's for me, for me!' Kathy yelled.

'Don't be silly, Kathy,' Rachel said, answering the call. They had never stopped Kathy's school friends from telephoning, but the last time it had been a boy on the line; another thing Rachel felt she must cope with before it developed.

This time it was a man. A responsible man. Rachel listened to what he had to say, with growing bewilderment. She was hardly aware that Neil had come out and was standing by her side.

'But I don't understand,' he heard her say.

'What is it?' he muttered to Rachel.

She covered the receiver with her hand. 'Someone from a school of music in London who says he's interested in Kathy, through a recommendation – what can that mean? The school?'

'Well, ask him,' Neil said, not being able to see Kathy's red face.

Rachel talked some more, and then hung up. 'He wants to come and see us. He's apparently in the district, staying with friends.'

174

'Better let him come, then,' Neil said. Unlike Rachel, he hadn't much patience with Kathy, but if the girl had talent and someone was going to pay for her to be taught, he wasn't personally going to stand in her way.

'What did he say?' Kathy clamoured.

'He said he'd heard that you were good at the piano and he wanted to arrange for you to be taught. In London,' Rachel said slowly. 'But that isn't the way it's done. If we'd applied, and got an appointment for you to go to London for an audition and there was a free scholarship being offered, I could understand it.'

'But you wouldn't let any kind rich person settle me in a school of music, would you?' Kathy stormed. 'No, you want to hold me back. She's right! She says you want to keep everyone down because you've got no talents yourself.'

'Who was right?' Rachel asked icily, but she knew the answer before it came. Dr Fenton.

'She's kind and understanding,' Kathy stormed. 'One day when everyone was out, she asked me to play to her and she said I was absolutely wizard at it and she could see me being a concert pianist only I'd have to go away from this house and stay in London where there'd be peace and–'

'Be quiet, Kathy!' Rachel snapped, trying

175

to think. 'Her again! But why, why? Neil, can you see why? She's just tearing the fabric of this home apart, but *why?*'

'You're stupid,' Kathy stormed. 'Who cares about the fabric of this home as you grandly call it? What's so special about this? I shall be in her London flat, and wearing nice clothes and I shall be a concert pianist and travel abroad and you don't like that. You won't let me have my chance. You want to hold me back.'

'Kathy, don't you see–?' Rachel pleaded.

'No, I don't see! You've got no rights in me. I shall ask my brother what to do. He'll make you let me go – what did you bring me here for, anyway? To train me to do housework for you, to be an unpaid servant–'

'Oh, really, Kathy, now you're being absurd!' Rachel exploded. 'In the first place you invited yourself here and cried when you were supposed to go home again. There was nobody there, no comfort, nothing. And you *are* related to us so why shouldn't you stay with us if you wanted to? As to being trained for housework, why, you'd never even consent to do a bit of washing up!'

'No, and I'm not going to, and I *will* go to London–'

'You won't, you know,' Rachel said, with tight lips. 'It's none of Dr Fenton's business, and I say you're not to go. You'll stay here under my eye until you're eighteen.'

Kathy yelled, 'I won't! Just try and stop me!' and tore upstairs. They could hear her banging about in her room. Mrs Pym said, 'What was all that about?' as she looked out of the kitchen door. Deirdre wheeled herself from the dining-room where she had been setting the table and looked at Rachel with raised eyebrows. 'Not very well managed, was it?' she said.

Neil, unexpectedly, snapped at Deirdre. 'Rachel has enough to put up with, without your unsolicited comments, Deirdre. Mind your own business!' To Rachel, he said, 'Come in – there's something I want to tell you, Rachel.'

'Oh, have you two made it up, then?' Deirdre said slowly, and came as near to a sneer as her sweet face would allow. 'Charlie Roberts closing the ranks together, I take it.'

'That will do, Deirdre!' Neil snapped, and shut the door on her.

'What is it, Neil?' Rachel asked, in a spent voice.

'Yes, you're tired and over-worked, and I haven't helped by quarrelling with you,' he said. 'I'm sorry, old girl. But in the dark place I'm locked in, it looked different. But not any more. The thing is, I don't think you managed that too well. No, don't turn on me – listen, if you will. Personally I think it would be a good thing if Dr Fenton did do something useful like that for a change.

She's made enough trouble so far.'

'Yes, but *is* it useful? I feel there's something behind it, Neil. And I want to know why she should. It isn't in reason. Quite clearly she will be paying for it, and why should she? Kathy isn't all that good, I'm quite sure of that, and what is more, she's undisciplined and won't ever submit to the discipline of a musical career, let alone things like good manners and being easy to live with. And why should we be under such an obligation to Dr Fenton?'

'There is that about it,' Neil agreed, but there was that in his voice which suggested to the sharply listening Rachel that his usual big bump of pride was missing. He was like a small desperate animal nuzzling around in the dark, searching for something with a frightening desperation. 'But there's more to it than that. I have the vague, tormenting idea that it's something to do with the accident.'

'The accident! How do you mean, Neil?'

'I can't find words to put it to you, Rachel. It's more like an instinctive feeling. I keep remembering that accident, and wondering why things turned out like that. There are so many facets to it. I think Deirdre could help to clarify things, if she would.'

'But why are you going back to that, Neil? What has that to do with Dr Fenton's making such havoc in this family?'

'I don't know,' Neil said slowly. 'It's like an elusive shadow. Something I *feel*. I felt it when I heard Trent's voice.'

'Max Trent? You mean you've met him before?' Rachel was surprised.

'I don't know. Describe him again to me, Rachel.'

So she did. But the playboy type she presented didn't help. Max Trent had no special feature of face that she could have pinned down. If he had had a big nose, she thought, or a particularly engaging grin, or a mannerism, anything, to make a word-picture for the sightless Neil. But Max Trent hadn't; he was like a tailor's dummy, with as much personality. Middle-of-the-way. A playboy type who, apart from the fact that his tweed suit had seen better days and had once been very good, conformed to the fashion of clothes, hair style, way of speaking, of every other young man of his kind who went around in that sort of low-slung car.

Neil said again, 'It was his voice. It rang a bell, somewhere. I think it was either before or at the time of the accident.'

'You mean he could be another witness?' Rachel asked eagerly.

Neil's voice was bitter as he said, 'Witness! We don't want any more of those. The ones we had were so ready to believe that it was my fault as much as the driver's, so how do witnesses help.'

Rachel's silence hit out at him. He turned on her. 'Rachel, didn't even *you* believe me? Heavens, when I think back. There I was, walking along that stretch of road, never swerving for one moment. Just walking neatly on the pavement, well away from the kerb, thinking my own thoughts. (Yes, and I can even remember them! I was thinking about Charlie Roberts and that new friend of his, and I was also thinking that Charlie's friend might possibly know that chap Clinton who had escaped from prison that week. They'd be in the district I was walking in, I thought – and I was right, as things later turned out.) My hunches, my instincts, are not often wrong, Rachel.'

'Only when they're about me, and the things you think I do to hurt you, Neil,' she said. She couldn't help saying that.

'We've put that matter to one side,' he told her gently, 'but from my point of view, and fed with a liberal dose of brain-washing by Dr Fenton, I think it was inevitable that I should think so. But that's done. We're discussing the accident, and Dr Fenton didn't get at me to brainwash me and I know very well that I didn't turn suddenly to cross the road and make those two cars crash head-on in an effort to avoid me.'

'I know you can say that, Neil dear, but the witness was looking at you. And you

180

could have been confused'

'No, Rachel, I was not confused. I didn't move from the centre of the pavement. If you remember, I was *found* on the centre of the pavement. One of the cars mounted the pavement, knocked me down and went off the pavement again.'

'But there were no skid marks, Neil,' she said painfully.

'And I believe someone persuaded a witness to talk, for some reason,' he muttered. 'Charlie Roberts' friend, because I was very close to finding the chap everyone wanted to find? I don't know. Anyway, it doesn't matter now, because they caught him eventually. But it did matter very much to our hope of any compensation. Don't you see, Rachel?'

'But if you could find out, Neil, wouldn't it be too late to do anything about the compensation now?'

'That isn't the point,' he said doggedly. 'I want to know how that all happened like that. That witness so conveniently being found, who was prepared to swear that I had done things to cause the accident, which I hadn't. And another thing, we still haven't found out who Deirdre was *with*. It's all very fine you saying we're not to worry her, Rachel, but it's a long time ago now, and if she admitted who she was with–'

'But he died, Neil, and it's too cruel to torture her with the memory of it now.

Besides, it wasn't his fault.'

'How do we know? It seems to me that perhaps Dr Fenton knew that chap, had an interest in him. I don't know. She's altogether too much interested in this family for my comfort, and she isn't making us any happier by her interest.'

'No, I have felt that,' Rachel admitted. 'But I can't think she had anything to do with the accident. I don't know what the reason is, except that some women just don't like other women, and she doesn't like me. You won't believe this, but I heard her persuading my boss's husband to chuck everything up here and go to London and open up a smart salon and she even offered to lend him the money to do it. What about that?'

'There you are, you see!' Neil said in near triumph. 'A born mischief-maker. And I'll tell you something else. Something I didn't tell Dr Ingram when he was asking about her interest in me. I think she was a jolly sight too quick off the mark in taking my case over and in saying that nothing could be done. Well, we're alone, aren't we? I can tell you what I think about it, can't I?'

He had heard Rachel catch her breath in surprise. He said sharply, 'Well, we *are* alone, aren't we?'

'Yes, oh, yes,' she said, distractedly. 'It's just that I was counting up the things in my mind that Dr Fenton had touched, spoilt, since she first saw me in the hairdresser's. She's made Deirdre discontented and suspicious, too. Deirdre has stopped working for The Gift Shop.'

She wished she hadn't said that. It made Neil look all uncertain again, baffled, angry in a helpless way. She shouldn't have worried him. 'I must go up and soothe Kathy's ruffled feathers, I suppose. Neil, you're not going to let her go to London with that woman, are you?'

Neil wouldn't answer. His lips shut in a tight line again, so Rachel went upstairs to find Kathy and try to talk her out of wanting to go. But in the event, it didn't happen. Kathy was nowhere to be found, and neither was Felicity. Both their rooms looked as if a tornado had gone through them. Rachel was surveying the damage when Mrs Pym joined her. Mrs Pym stood silently, but not particularly surprised.

Rachel looked searchingly at her. Mrs Pym said, 'So that was what it was all about! Gone, both of them. Whispering and creaking down the stairs and bumping their cases on the banisters as they went. I thought it was just another caper but I got called away and then everything was quiet and it slipped my mind. Well, they won't have got far, dear, because they've got no money. Heard them saying so.'

'Mrs Pym, for a woman of your age, you have very little sense at times,' Rachel said heatedly. 'The lack of money wouldn't stop Kathy – she'd take a taxi straight to Dr Fenton and leave her to pay for it, or she'd shamelessly accept a lift on a lorry, Felicity too. That child looks older than she is. Oh, what shall I do? It will have to be the police, I suppose, but I didn't want to do that.'

'You'll have to, duck, unless you want to call Dr Ingram. It's his ward, you know, as well as your young cousin,' Mrs Pym said sensibly.

'How long have they been gone?' Rachel asked breathlessly.

'About half an hour,' Mrs Pym said, thinking. 'I heard you and your cousin talking in the sitting-room, and your sister wheeled herself out into the hall to see what the commotion was, so I thought I wouldn't interfere.'

'Deirdre? She saw them go?' Rachel couldn't believe it so she dashed into the dining-room where she had last seen her sister.

'Deirdre!' Rachel cried out. 'Mrs Pym says you saw Kathy and Felicity running away. Is that true?'

Deirdre shrugged. 'I saw them going downstairs, looking very conspiratorial. I thought it was some new silly game.'

'Oh, Deirdre, how could you? Why didn't

you tell me?'

'Because,' Deirdre said sweetly, 'you shut me out. You went into that room to talk privately with Neil. Well, you can't have it all ways. Dr Fenton says you make favourites and play one person off against another, and it's true. You do!'

'If I hear that woman's name once more, I shall – I shall get very angry!' Rachel exploded. 'Deirdre, what have I done to you that you should turn from me, to a stranger you never even liked?'

'A person can make a mistake, I suppose,' Deirdre said stiffly. 'Anyway, Dr Fenton is going to have me looked at again. She thinks she knows someone, private and personal, who can do something for me. Someone important, in a nursing home.'

'Oh, really, and who is going to pay for this?' Rachel was stung to enquire.

'*She* is,' Deirdre said quickly. 'She isn't as bad as you've always made out. I've seen my mistake, oh, yes, I've seen how I always looked to you to boss everyone around and I thought I was doing the right thing, letting you run my life. I can see I was so wrong.'

'But such a little while ago you were just aching to get home from hospital because you said she had no interest in you and made you feel as if you were a nuisance,' Rachel marvelled.

'She's very busy,' Deirdre said, leaping to

185

Dr Fenton's defence, 'and she doesn't get much help from Dr Ingram. It's true what she says – since you got your claws into him, he's like a man bemused. He neglects his work and his friends and he neglects her. You didn't know, did you, that they had an understanding before you even met him? But you wouldn't care about coming between two people, would you?' Tears started to pour down her cheeks and she breathed too fast. Rachel moved towards her, to help her, but Deirdre shouted, 'Don't touch me! Don't pretend to be a ministering angel to me – keep that act for your dear Dr Ingram!'

Rachel halted in her tracks. 'Dr Ingram – I must telephone him about Felicity. Oh, let me think, where can I find him at this moment?'

'Don't pretend you don't know,' Deirdre couldn't help thrusting at her. Rachel shut the door on her sister's voice, and tried to think. The hospital would tell her where he was, if he wasn't on duty. Most likely in the Path Lab with his friend, the professor.

But at that moment Boyd Ingram was with Thora Fenton, in her flat. Thora was defending Kathy and Felicity, and doing it well. 'They don't like her, but they haven't made a fuss about it. She keeps rigid rules, in spite of all you say about her, and makes their lives a perfect misery, as only a girl who is music-mad can be made miserable.'

'Not Mrs Roberts,' Boyd Ingram said, in astonishment. 'You *can't* be talking about *her!* She's such a good, understanding soul.'

Thora looked pityingly at him. 'She's fooled you, too, has she? I think that's wicked. You're such a fine man, all that's good, and she had no right to do this. I'm not the only one who sees her for what she is, you know. Even her own sister Deirdre has turned against her. You didn't know that, did you?'

'Deirdre? Turned against Rachel Roberts? Oh, what rot,' Boyd said roundly. 'Really, Thora, you must be losing that good sense I always admired in you. Why, they're the most devoted family.'

'Neil too?' Thora murmured. 'Does he still like Rachel Roberts as much as he did at one time?' And she saw to her satisfaction that Boyd hesitated. 'Yes, I can see you're thinking again on that score. I've watched that astute young man putting two and two together. He doesn't know what to do, he's helpless, blind as he is. But I intend to do something for him. Oh, I know I said I couldn't see any hope at one time, but I've remembered Forsdyke. He ought to be interested in the case. He returned from America last week. And to prove to you how sincere I am, I'm going to see that Neil gets any treatment without cost to him at all.'

Boyd frowned at her. She said, 'You don't

believe me. I can see you have been talked over by that Rachel Roberts. Oh, she's got a glib tongue all right. I daresay she's told you I wasn't very nice to Deirdre. That's been going the rounds – I've heard it. Well, I suppose you won't be impressed when I tell you I've found someone at last to consider her case. Of course, I may not be successful, and then I suppose everyone will revile me, as usual, the family of Deirdre in particular. But before that happens, you remember, Boyd, what I've said to you today.'

'You're so mistaken, Thora,' Boyd said worriedly. 'If you can do something for Neil and Deirdre, I shall be for ever your debtor, but I can't believe that Rachel will hold it against you if your efforts fail.'

'You're so generous to people, without always bothering to see what they're really like,' she said, smiling gently. 'And you do tend, dear Boyd, to go on face values. That family party over the toffee-apples quite threw you that day, didn't it? But I heard (from Deirdre, actually) that there had been an awful row just before that, and another one afterwards. We just happened to catch them doing something that looked nice. It isn't always like that.'

Boyd turned away angrily. Thora didn't know how many times he himself had dropped into that house and had found comfort and peace, and of how Rachel's influence was everywhere. Something had gone wrong in that house, he thought, and it was nothing to do with Rachel.

'I'll tell you something else you won't like, Boyd,' Thora said. 'I've hesitated to worry you with it. I've tried to settle it myself but it's been difficult. Young Felicity goes out with boys. Oh, I know she's only thirteen, but Kathy is easily led, considering she's the elder, and nobody watches them. I really do feel that Rachel ought to be aware of a girl of thirteen getting out of the house late at night. I've seen her myself standing at the corner talking to boys. But Rachel just doesn't bother.'

He swung round on his heel. 'Thora, you can't realize what you're saying! A girl of thirteen, getting out of the house – *my niece?*'

'She looks quite seventeen, Boyd, with all that make-up on. You probably haven't seen it.' And she was rewarded by the baffled look again. He had heard all this from Hazel next door.

'I've done my best to help Kathy,' Thora went on. 'I've got a man interested in her music. Phelps, at that big new place in London. The girl's mad keen to go. They won't let her practise because of Neil's stupid writing, and you know, he isn't any good – his work gets rejected, you know that, don't you? – but it has to come first, not Kathy's music. But no, Rachel has refused to let her go to London, even though it's to be at my expense.'

Boyd turned to her. 'All this at your expense, Thora? But why, why – have you any idea how much all this is going to cost you?'

'Oh, yes. I've thought. Perhaps it's because I don't like to see wrong going unrighted. Perhaps it's because I had a vague thought that it would please you, Boyd. I don't know. I can't always explain myself what I feel, but I can't expect you to appreciate that, my dear, can I? You think I'm so hard, don't you? Well, perhaps all this will persuade you that I'm not!'

'But I still don't see–' he began, looking at her more in puzzlement than pleasure. 'Won't other people wonder why you're being so handsomely generous to this particular family, Thora?'

She struggled to keep the friendly smile in place on her face. 'It was the last thing I expected to hear you say, Boyd. I don't know what I really did expect to hear you say, except that perhaps you would consider letting me have your niece for a while. She really *is* a handful, but at my home, there are so many people who could take her in hand.' She put a hand on his. 'Boyd, break away from the influence of Mrs Roberts. Get Felicity away from her, too. I'm a woman, and I can see through her. You're not the first man to be taken in by her. After all,' she said, with something of a master stroke, 'she was rather deceitful about that husband of hers, wasn't she? And she's still denying his existence, I hear.'

It caught him on the raw. That had been the one thing he hadn't understood. Rachel had been so open and frank about everything, but whenever he had tried to find out about the husband, she had shied away from the subject. Even now, the subject of the man was still shrouded in mystery. And in that unhappy moment, Rachel telephoned.

Thora got up leisurely and answered it. He wasn't looking at her or he would have seen the naked dislike in her face for an instant as she recognized Rachel's voice. 'Boyd,' Thora said softly, covering the receiver, 'it's Mrs Roberts and she insists on speaking to you. Do you want to talk to her?'

'Wants me? Here?' he asked, and tried to make his legs take him slowly across the room to the telephone. His mind coldly told him that what Thora had been saying about Rachel had the ring of truth in it, but his whole being wanted to leap to Rachel's side, instinctively to protect her from everyone, particularly Thora.

Rachel's opening words dispelled this sensation, however. 'Boyd,' she said urgently, 'I've been searching everywhere for you and the hospital put me on to you here. I'm in a

terrible fix. I don't know how to say it.
Kathy's run away and Felicity has gone with
her!'

Chapter Seven

Boyd looked at his niece with no great liking. It was as Thora had said: with the make-up and the clothes (and heaven knew where they came from!) she looked every bit seventeen. It took a lot to frighten him but this child of his sister's really did make him apprehensive. He felt he couldn't let her go out of his sight without anxiety. Heaven knew what would happen to her.

'Go and wash that stuff off your face!' he thundered. 'You, too, Kathy. I'll pay off the taxi.'

'And I'll telephone Mrs Roberts to tell her they've turned up,' Thora said, suiting the action to the words. Without actually making a stand in front of those youngsters with the knowledgeable eyes, Boyd didn't feel he could do much to stop her, so he marched out, intending to call Rachel up later. He didn't hear what Thora said to her.

Rachel put the telephone down, after a scorching two minutes. She found Neil at her elbow. 'Well, the girls are found. They went straight to Dr Fenton's flat in a taxi and Dr Ingram was there and has gone down to pay the cabby. And Dr Fenton enjoyed herself, telling me what she thought of me. So now we know.'

'What exactly did she say, Rachel?' Neil's voice had an edge to it.

'Enough,' Rachel said shortly. 'From which I may take it that Felicity won't be coming back, and that means Mrs Pym will go too.'

Mrs Pym was, of course, listening. She came out into the hall, her eyes wet. 'Did Dr Ingram say I must go, Rachel, dear?' she said.

'Oh, you're listening in again! Well, if I don't tell you, dear Dr Fenton will,' Rachel said bitterly. 'It seems that Felicity won't be entrusted to me any longer, so of course, he won't be paying you to be here. It's as simple as that.'

'But I've got nowhere else to go,' Mrs Pym said, in a frightened voice. 'Besides, I like it here. I like being with you, Rachel dear. Can't I stay? Just for my roof and board? I'll work for them.'

Rachel relented, and smiled at her, but shook her head. 'Oh, Mrs Pym – you don't know. You don't know the half of it. I won't have a penny to bless myself with, let alone feed you. And Neil has lost so much by that work going astray.'

Mrs Pym said shrewdly, 'And there'll be all that money you'll be paying that nasty young man who came here and says he's your husband.'

Neil drew a sharp breath and Rachel

looked dismayed.

'Don't mind me, dear. The minute I saw him go into the sitting-room that day, I said to myself, that's a wrong 'un. You can tell. Don't you give him anything, dear. You'll be sorry. He'll come back and back, again and again.'

'You mind your own business,' Deirdre snapped, from the other side of the hall, where she emerged from the kitchen silently in that chair of hers. 'It just doesn't concern you and I wish you'd go away from here.'

'What's got into you, Deirdre, to talk to Mrs Pym like that?' Rachel gasped. 'You never used to be like this!'

'If you ask me, it's a touch of Dr Fenton-itis,' Mrs Pym said. 'Nice as pie to the young people, that woman is, but I've felt the lash of her tongue before now, I can tell you! I've been in hospital, and you don't always get dear Dr Ingram to look after you, more's the pity.'

'Well, Deirdre isn't to talk to you like that,' Rachel insisted. 'Don't worry about staying here for the time being, Mrs Pym. You know the money position, but you can stay if you don't mind going short with the rest of us. You agree, Neil?'

'Yes, I agree,' Neil said slowly. He was far away, living over again in his mind, that accident. He had thought a lot about it lately, since Dr Fenton had come into their

195

home and their private lives, and the elusive factor he kept almost reaching, still kept slipping away before he had caught hold of it. He said, 'Mrs Pym, you'd be the one to post my stuff for me, when Rachel's not here. You wouldn't let anyone else take it from you, would you?'

Deirdre rose to the bait. 'Well, Kathy didn't, either. At least—'

'At least … what?' Neil said coldly.

Deirdre had always been a little in awe of Neil. He had lost a lot of his bloom of youth when he had taken over the responsibility of the family at twenty. He was two years Rachel's senior and had always maintained that he was the man of the family, and he alone could make Deirdre do as he wished, until he had lost his sight and some of his authority. Now, oddly, his anger gave him that old authority back. Deirdre wilted, and said, 'I didn't mean to say it. Well, what I mean is, at least it wasn't planned. She didn't keep your letters back purposely.'

'Who are you talking about? *Kathy?*' Neil thundered. 'Or Dr Fenton?'

'How did you know?' Deirdre faltered, without reckoning on Neil's anger giving him an inspired guess. 'Kathy was out in her car with her and Eileen saw her and thought she'd get to the post first, being in a car. Besides, being your relative … well, it was natural for Eileen to give them to her. Only

196

Dr Fenton said she had to go somewhere first and they'd have plenty of time to go to the chief sorting office, only it somehow never came off and Kathy forgot.'

Neil walked back into the sitting-room. Rachel followed him. 'But why, why should she do such a thing? Such a little petty thing?'

'It's all of a piece,' he said. 'On the one hand she holds out the hope of a cure for me, a cure for Deirdre, a musical career for Kathy – and on the other hand she takes away my living by an astute trick like that, and she keeps you from Ingram by a lucky break, finding Charlie Roberts. (Well, if she hadn't come across him, I daresay she wouldn't have been above paying someone to act the part, you having given her the framework by that stupid lie about being married). And do you know what I think? She wants Ingram, and she wants to make us so dependent on her that we'll never be able to turn around on her for what's she guilty of. We shan't be able to say a word.'

'Am I very stupid, Neil?' Rachel whispered. 'I don't think I know what she *is* guilty of?'

'I think she can have the accident laid at her door … in some way,' Neil said, very softly, so that only Rachel heard. 'I don't know how. I can't just think. Sometimes I'm tempted to believe she was in the car that

197

ran up on the pavement and knocked me down. Sometimes I can't accept that. But somehow, in some way, she has an interest in people not knowing the truth about it.'

'But she wouldn't ... I mean, she couldn't.' Rachel couldn't get out what she did mean. 'She's a doctor, an important person at the hospital, known locally...'

'And wouldn't you think that with all that, she wouldn't stoop to such things as she's doing to us?' Neil took her up. 'But thinking about it, it is that very reputation of hers that wouldn't let people recognize what she's doing, even if they noticed. They just wouldn't think of it of her. And there must be a big reason, and that must be the only one. Now Rachel, I want you to do something. Go and look up the old local newspapers of that time. Something might be in them that everyone missed the significance of then, but which might mean something now.'

'Yes, Neil, after I come from work. I must go now,' Rachel said worriedly, looking at her watch.

Samara York was waiting for her. She was angry about something, which was unusual. Rachel said, 'Is anything wrong? I'm sorry I didn't get here on time but everything has gone to pieces at our house.'

Samara York shook her head. 'No, don't take any notice of me, dear. It's just that Dr Fenton.'

Rachel threw up her head. 'You, too? She's the one who has upset us! But how could she have bothered you? I thought she was a valued customer!'

'She isn't a customer of long standing,' Samara York said severely. She was a smallish woman, indomitable, and very plain, but by her very disposition, the plain face was filled with character and didn't seem so plain. She played up to it by using chalk white make-up, so that her severely dressed black hair, black brows and dark eyes, were dramatic, and her lipstick was the only splash of colour. Today her eyes snapped angrily as she said, 'and a customer such as that can very well be dispensed with when it's a question of making everybody else unhappy.'

Rachel looked receptive and Mrs York said more than she had intended. 'She has been persuading my husband to cut from the business and go it alone in London. If he did that, it would ruin us both financially, and break up our marriage, too. If anyone thinks such a customer is needed–'

Rachel bit her lip. She knew only too well the truth of that. She had heard part of that particular conversation between Dr Fenton and Raoul. But there was no point in letting her employer feel that she had been the last to know what was going on. So Rachel said slowly, 'She's a mischief-maker, it seems.

199

She has caused great trouble in our house, playing off one against another.'

'She's a family friend of yours?' Mrs York asked in consternation.

'Oh, no! Indeed, I can't think why she took us up, except that Dr Ingram started to come here, because he was interested in Deirdre – my sister, you know, who is a patient at the hospital still. He came two or three times, and then Dr Fenton started to drop in with him, but more often without him, it seems.'

Mrs York looked unsatisfied. 'I don't know what I'm about, running her down to you,' she said, half to herself. 'I might have known, seeing the interest she took in you, and that money.'

'What money?' Rachel took her up swiftly.

Patchy colour flared in Mrs York's white cheeks and she looked really bothered. 'My tongue's running away with me,' she gasped. 'I'm in such a state I don't know what I'm saying!'

'You must tell me! It's terribly important because of another matter,' Rachel said, so heatedly that her employer capitulated.

'Oh, well, why should I care about her? Her and her extracting promises of silence from me,' she said to Rachel. 'She hasn't kept her part of the bargain. She *would* have Raoul do her hair and I ought to have known what that sort of woman would be like.'

'Yes, but *what* money, dear Mrs York?' Rachel insisted.

Samara York forced herself to concentrate. 'You didn't really think I could afford to run a bonus scheme like that, did you, dear, just for a girl in the reception desk? I mean, I thought from the first that you'd never swallow that story. I told her so at the time, but she said that if I was firm enough, you'd believe anything because you needed money so badly. Well, that's the long and short of it. I don't give any bonus, of course. It was her idea. She wanted you to have the money, regular, and she said you'd be too proud to take it from outsiders.'

'She said *wha-at?*'

'There was some tale about someone who was interested in the plight of you all – so many of you hurt in an accident and no adult to look after you all, so she said she'd been asked to feed the money to you regularly, but to make it look like something connected with your job.'

Rachel sat stunned, her mouth open a little in sheer surprise. Then she pulled herself together. 'Did *you* believe that story, Madame?'

Mrs York wriggled uncomfortably. 'Well, dear, to tell you the truth I didn't worry about it much at first. She was the first moneyed customer I'd had, and I'll own I thought she'd bring other people of her kind here, fool that I was. Well, that Dr Ingram came, and he seemed interested in you, and there was that young chap in the sports car asking for her, and I began to think–' She broke off, then said with determination, 'Besides, you do hear of kind people anonymously giving money to people who are hit by circumstances, and such young people, too, all on their own. Well, and it wasn't any of my business,' she finished lamely.

Rachel continued her work automatically, answering the telephone and making and breaking appointments with a frozen face and a cold frightened feeling inside her. Why, why, she kept asking herself, why did Dr Fenton do these things? For what reason could she possibly? Neil must be right – it must be to do with the accident.

She couldn't get away quickly enough that day, and ran for her bus to the newspaper offices. But she just missed it. Angrily, she began to run, with the idea of catching a train. The station was ten minutes away. Dr Ingram cruised along beside her in his car, pulling up when she saw him. 'Get in, Rachel. I'll take you where you want to go, but I want to talk to you, too.'

'No. No, thanks, I don't want a lift,' she said, her face set and her eyes dark and stormy with anger. He had never seen her like this.

'Please – I must talk to you,' he said, so,

because traffic was making protesting noises around him, and people were staring, she got in.

He said right away, 'I've got so much to talk to you about, I don't know where to begin. First, your cousin Kathy – do let her go to that music school in London. She'll be all right, I assure you.'

'No!' Rachel said, in a tight, frozen voice. 'Do you think I'd accept favours from you now? Or from Dr Fenton? Why couldn't you have spoken to me on the telephone, accepted my apology, *helped* me? Why did you leave me to *her*, to enjoy herself telling me what she thought of me?'

'Dr Fenton means well–' he began.

'No!' Rachel flared. 'And if that's what you want to say to me, then you can stop this car and let me get out.'

'But why are you so against her, Rachel? So suddenly?'

'Because it's all piled up suddenly, and I've realized what she's been doing to us. When you came in that last time, Neil and I were quarrelling bitterly over what she'd suggested to him about me. Since then, I've learned that Deirdre has been set against me by her. She's fired Kathy's very inflammable nature so that she's run out on me because I said no to accepting charity from Dr Fenton, regarding the music school. And only in the last hour or so, I've learned that it's Dr Fenton's money, not my employer's, that is providing the treasured "bonus" that helped us so much.'

'Oh, now, Rachel,' he said, pulling in to the side. 'Surely–!'

'Don't you try and defend her to me,' Rachel fumed. 'If you like her, you're welcome to her. Just send Kathy home, and let's finish it all. There's my bus – we've overtaken it,' and she ripped open the door, slammed it behind her, and ran. He watched her angry little figure as she jumped on the scarcely slowing down bus. She was so simmering with anger, even the conductor looked enquiringly at her. Rachel didn't care; she had caught her bus.

But that was her last piece of good luck. She drew a blank at the newspaper offices. She didn't remember reading much of inter-est at the time, but now, reading everything with a new interest, she could see that there was little to help them. The newspaper account was not Neil's – it was Dr Fenton's version, simply, baldly. The pedestrian started to run towards the first car that had crashed (and Rachel had to admit to herself that Neil would do just that, whether he had seen Deirdre in it or not) and the second car bounced away, away from the first car and towards Neil, who literally ran right into it. It did admit that the young woman (Deirdre) was thrown out, and run over by another car who couldn't help himself. Why, Rachel thought, hadn't Deirdre got compensation, for something that hadn't been her fault? And then a later account produced a witness who said that Deirdre had been trying to make the driver stop, and she had thrown open her door and jumped out; in which case it was her liability, Rachel thought wretchedly.

She was lucky getting home. Their own local cab driver saw her and offered her a lift. He had finished for the day. He talked cheerfully about his wife's new baby, and asked Rachel to come in to see it. He lived two doors away from her. But even he could see she wasn't in her usual, warmly smiling mood, and he dried up and whistled between his teeth for the rest of the way.

Somehow, Rachel thought, as she thanked him and promised to come and see his wife, somehow she must tell Neil what she had read in the newspaper files in such a way that it didn't upset him. How would it feel, she asked herself, to be in total darkness, and to hear such news, with no hope at all? She went on thinking all round this, while she laid tea. Neil was not there. He must have slipped out for a walk. Deirdre was in the kitchen with Mrs Pym but when she heard Rachel's step, she wheeled herself out, into her own small bedroom behind the kitchen. Rachel blinked sharp tears out of her eyes and went on laying the table. Someone came in at the unlocked front door. Rachel gladly went towards it, saying, 'Is that you, Neil?'

But it wasn't Neil. It was Charlie Roberts.

He swaggered in, malicious laughter filling his eyes, his fair hair crisping up into tight waves with the oil he had combed into it. He was so handsome, it hit you in the eye, Rachel thought bitterly. And he knew it.

'What do *you* want?' she said. She knew, of course. He was back for the promised money, and she had given herself the pleasure of telling Samara York that she would touch no more of it. Samara York hardly expected her to, she could see that. They shared fully their loathing of Dr Fenton. It would be the new bond that held employer and employed together. Rachel said, with a certain amount of satisfaction, 'If it's money, you're out of luck. There isn't any, now I come to add up.'

Charlie's smile slipped for one minute, and one minute only. He recovered and said easily, 'Oh, naughty, naught, fancy thinking such a thing of your lovely husband. I don't want *money*, only my rights and comforts,' and he lounged easily across the room towards her.

He was a big man, and the room was too cluttered for Rachel, slender as she was, to slip out of his way. He clutched her to him and took great hurting angry kisses, greedy kisses, of her soft mouth. Between them she screamed, and kicked out at him. His anger grew with her efforts. It wasn't a pretty scene. Deirdre could hear it in her room, and after a brief struggle with her herself, she came out, wheeling her chair round the awkward turn with difficulty. But her action stopped Mrs Pym from coming to help Rachel. It was Neil who got there first, quietly coming in at the open front door, his keen hearing telling him what had happened.

He didn't stop to think what he could do. In times past, he would have plucked Charlie Roberts away, and punished him with short shift and the scientific knowledge he had. Now he was blind, and could only be guided by his ears. He found Charlie Roberts' jersey, expecting the officers' jacket which would have helped. The jersey just stretched. So he found Charlie's ears and hung on to them, anything to get him away from Rachel, without hurting her. Hurting Rachel by ineffectual blows from his own hands, worried Neil more than anything.

Charlie let out a howl of pain and rage, let go of Rachel, and despite her scream of warning to Neil, Charlie threw him across the room, with one blow of his powerful arm. Neil's head hit the wall and he sank, like a limp outsize rag doll, on to the floor.

Sharp silence held everything still for a second, then Rachel said, in a horrified voice, 'You've killed him. He's *dead!*'

Charlie looked sick as he glanced at the chalk white face of Neil. In foreign ports this sort of thing happened, and Charlie had one remedy. He usually got out, quick, and he didn't come back. This he tried to do now. Mrs Pym, fluttering in the doorway, flattened herself to the wall as he tore past, but Deirdre, in her invalid chair, couldn't get out of his way so easily. He cannoned into it, leaving the house with a thud of footsteps that had a curious ring of finality to them. Rachel, cuddling Neil's inert form in her arms, felt that it was the end of everything for them.

She couldn't remember much afterwards of the next few minutes. Only her impassioned grief at what happened to Neil, who so unthinkingly leapt in to help her, blind as he was. Mrs Pym's insistent shaking of her shoulder, made Rachel look up. 'Look at your sister,' Mrs Pym begged.

She stared blindly through her tears, hardly hearing what it was Mrs Pym was saying. Mrs Pym was being so insistent. It came to Rachel that she must get up and telephone for the ambulance. Hurt person, ambulance, in that order. Her stunned brain was making an effort to work again.

She gently put Neil down on the ground

again and dragged herself to her feet. The room was a shambles. At the door, Mrs Pym hovering at her elbow, she got her first sight of the over-turned invalid chair. Mrs Pym's hand was on her arm, squeezing it, warningly. Deirdre had somehow dragged herself clear, and was now on her feet, pulling herself along by the banister rails, forcing her feet, one after the other, to move, towards the telephone. She stared at the telephone as she made painful effort after painful effort. It was the Mecca for Deirdre. For perhaps the first time for a long time now, Rachel recalled that her sister had once been a student nurse, a dedicated one.

Deirdre didn't reach the telephone. Someone else walked up the path, and Rachel knew those footsteps. Her heart started its wild unreasoning tattoo. It was always the same. There had never been anything she could do about it, even though she had felt herself to be unnoticed by him, unwanted, pushed out by Dr Fenton or by the fruits of her own stupid story about being a married woman. Now Boyd Ingram was here again, and her heart, at least, was registering a welcome.

But for Deirdre, it was interruption. She saw the door pushed open and she gave up the effort. Before Boyd's astonished eyes, she wavered on her weak legs and sank to the ground.

He rushed in. 'Deirdre! Whatever happened?' He saw the overturned chair before he caught sight of Rachel and Mrs Pym hiding round the corner. 'Are you hurt?'

'No. I walked,' Deirdre gasped. 'I did!'

And then reaction set in, and Deirdre collapsed, crying exhaustedly. Boyd put her chair upright and lifted her into it.

She pushed him away. 'Don't help me – it's Neil. Charlie Roberts killed him, I think. Get the ambulance!'

Rachel was at the telephone by then. Mrs Pym was fluttering around. 'Oh, doctor, such a terrible thing to have happened,' she sobbed, and it was she who told him what had been occurring in those last terrible minutes. Not Rachel. She asked for the ambulance in a frozen voice unlike her own, and she steadily ignored Boyd.

She looked very ill. There were dark smudges under her eyes, and her face had lost all its healthy colour and looked sunken.

After she had telephoned, he urged her to sit down. Mrs Pym made them all some good strong tea, well sweetened. Deirdre was quieter now. Boyd said she was to be kept quiet until he could get her, too, into the hospital. And then the ambulance came and Neil was taken away.

To Rachel, the hours went by on leaden feet. She had left Deirdre in Mrs Pym's charge, and sat solidly outside the ward where Neil had been taken. Someone came. A woman doctor. Rachel set her teeth so she wouldn't cry out if it were Dr Fenton, but it wasn't. It was an older woman, kind, pleasant; a doctor who said what she knew and what she didn't, and who had no axe to grind about Boyd Ingram. Boyd himself came soon afterwards. Rachel remembered him saying, 'He'll be all right, I think, Rachel. Why don't you go home?' but she had just shaken her head and stayed there.

A little later on Boyd came to tell her that Deirdre had been fetched and admitted. He was afraid she had hurt her hip in the fall when the chair went over, but he didn't tell Rachel that.

Later still, he came to tell her that Neil would be seeing a famous eye specialist first thing in the morning. She did look up then, and he said quietly, 'My dear, it's very late,' and he turned his watch round to her range of vision so she could see. 'Eleven o'clock. When did you eat last?'

She thought about it. 'Lunch time, I think, but it doesn't matter.'

'Oh, yes, it does. Put your coat on and come with me. There's a place where we can get a decent supper and have that talk. Now don't protest again – I'm afraid you'll be sorry if you don't. It's about something you want to know.'

Boyd always went to the sort of hotel

where from the doorstep one had nothing to do any more, not even to think, the service was so good. Rachel thought it resentfully, but the resentment ebbed away a little later when, with good food, some choice wine, warmth and the sense of being looked after, she could review things more calmly. She even managed to thank him civilly for his care of her.

'That's better,' he approved. 'That's more like my Rachel.'

She glanced at him, sparks in her eyes. 'No, don't fly off the handle at me again, my dear,' he begged her. 'Let me talk first.'

She shrugged. He took it to mean agreement and said, 'You went to the newspaper offices today. Now don't get angry – I too was going there, and I could have taken you if you'd only had a little patience with me.'

'Why did you want to go there? To see if your friend Dr Fenton was fully covered?' she flared, but before the look in his eyes, she cooled down and apologized. 'I'm sorry, but I've taken enough today. And now we find there's nothing to help us. We had to see again those papers, but it's all wrong. They found witnesses to say it was Neil's fault, and Deirdre's, and it wasn't. Neil said so and I believe him.'

'And so do I. Oh, don't cry, my dear, I can't bear it. And don't keep saying things to me about Dr Fenton. I am not on her side, as you put it. You must accept that. I am not on her side!'

'But you're friends, you two!' Rachel protested indignantly. 'She gave me to understand that you were engaged to be married, or going to be, and you wouldn't listen each time I tried to tell you I wasn't married.'

'Ah, yes, that matter. Well, since you've brought it up yourself, perhaps we'd better deal with that first. What *was* the truth of it, Rachel?' and he stared fixedly at the ring on her third finger.

Angrily she tugged it off, and dropped it in the ash tray. 'It isn't even a proper ring,' she said, bitterly. 'And it doesn't matter any more. I shall leave that job, but what I shall do, I can't think.' She started to shiver again. 'I used to be so sure of myself. I could fix everything. But now I don't know. I don't know anything any more. What will happen to Deirdre? What about Neil? How shall I cope?'

He reached over and covered one of her hands with his, and in spite of her struggles to get it away, he held on to it. 'You've got me. I'm your friend, do you hear, for as long as you want it that way.'

'Why? Why should you feel like that about me?' she flashed.

He hesitated. 'The day I met you at that reception desk in the hairdressers, I had been bedevilled with shyness. It's the most awful thing for a man. Oh, I could talk to the patients, and to colleagues, but the social scene terrified me. That changed when I met you. I don't know how. You gave me something, and nothing was the same again. Don't you think that's a good basis for a friendship?'

'You can't be friends with me *and* Dr Fenton. She won't have it. You should only see what she's done to us because of it.'

'It's over, that friendship – Dr Fenton knows it,' he said earnestly. 'And on the telephone, she said more to you than she should have. I hurried down to pay the taxi the girls came in, and I was going to speak to you then, but she'd hung up.'

'What about Kathy?' Rachel asked, a catch in her voice as she deliberately changed the subject. 'When can she come home? I don't want her to go to London.'

'Very well, she won't go, if you don't wish it,' he said reluctantly. 'At the moment she's at my home, with Felicity.' He looked displeased, so Rachel, misconstruing, said, 'Send Kathy home. I'm sure it will be for the best all round. Your family will loathe having her.'

'Never mind Kathy – what happened about her brother tonight?' he asked, getting to the point he wanted, rather ruthlessly.

'I can't tell you,' Rachel choked.

'Then I shall ask Neil, as soon as he's able to talk.'

'No! No, please don't do that.' She sighed. 'I've told you so often, I just made it up about being married. It was a stupid thing to do, but I was desperate for that job. I used Kathy's surname. It was a family one. It didn't seem to matter. Her brother was ... away at sea. He'd always been a nuisance to us. It had been a relief to see the back of him. Only he must have got into trouble aboard because he jumped ship at Marseilles and came back overland. To the hospital where Dr Fenton discovered him. You won't like this, but he told us she suggested to him that he come to us. As my husband.'

'But why?' he asked. The question Rachel and Neil had asked.

'I don't know why – or even what happened, but she must have seen that he's always wanting money. Well, we promised him money to go away and leave us alone. There was a bonus I got from my employer.'

She flushed and looked acutely embarrassed, while Boyd Ingram said a few angry things about men like Charlie Roberts who importuned women like Rachel herself. She shook her head.

'Not the point,' she choked. 'The point is, in collecting the bonus I found out that it wasn't from my employer at all but from Dr Fenton.'

She had some difficulty in making Boyd Ingram believe that. She told him how she had found out about it, and why her employer had betrayed the trust put in her by Thora Fenton.

'So when Charlie came tonight for money and I said there wasn't any, he said it didn't matter, he'd … take something else.' She looked down at her free hand stabbing the table with her fork. Her cheeks were stained bright red, and she still tried to get her other hand away from Boyd's grasp. At last she looked up and found him unaccountably angry. 'Well, it's over now,' she said. 'In the past. He won't come back, all the while he thinks he killed Neil. I know Charlie.'

'But supposing he does?' Boyd murmured, at last. 'I can't leave you in that house, with just Mrs Pym for company. You will permit me to arrange for her to stay there, by the way? I've nowhere else to send her, supposing you're too stiff-necked to want any part of my arranging.'

That drew a brief smile to her lips, but it soon fled. 'I'll be glad for her to stay. She's already asked if she can, and I told her I had no money, but it didn't matter. She wants to stay with us,' Rachel said.

'That's fine. Then we must get you a watchdog of some sort, since I'm well aware that you'd never listen to the other plan I have for your protection,' he said, in an odd voice.

'What is that, Dr Ingram?' she said stiffly, all prepared to refute it on the instant.

He said ruefully, 'If we're back to formal terms, Miss Arden, then of course it would be pointless for me to make any such suggestion. Now, about your sister Deirdre,' he rushed on, and talked about arrangements that had been made for her to be under the care of a friend of Boyd's, a specialist.

'Not Dr Fenton?' Rachel asked, in a relieved voice.

'Not Dr Fenton,' he assured her.

'Was it … just a freak, my sister managing to take a few steps tonight?' she asked, painfully.

'I don't know,' he said, after some thought. 'I would think – but I mustn't raise your hopes. Just have faith, my dear girl, just hang on.'

He took her home then. On the way, she said again, 'What *about* Kathy? When will she come home?'

After a short silence, he said, 'I'm going to be rather heavy-handed here, Rachel. I don't want her to go home. She'll worry about you. She's very head-strong. Besides, if Roberts does turn up again, it might be unpleasant for a girl of her age. Heaven knows I hope he won't turn up. To that end, I'm asking a friend of mine to keep a watch on the house.'

'You're *wha-at?*' she gasped.

'He's a policeman. A plain clothes man. He's game to do anything for me like that, because of his deep gratitude in a little matter of an ulcer which we cured. Not to worry. Just leave him to his job and feel comfortable. Get some sleep. That's what you need. And if you want to know why I'm doing this, it's to give me a bit of peace, too,' and, with a smile, he wouldn't allow any more to be said.

Mrs Pym wanted to know what had been happening at the hospital. Rachel endeavoured to edit a lot of what had been said between Boyd and herself, but Mrs Pym was no fool. 'Why don't you accept that dear man's offer of friendship?' Mrs Pym scolded. 'You could do a lot worse.'

'And a lot better,' Rachel said shortly. 'Dr Fenton will crack the whip tomorrow and he'll go running to her.'

'It seems to me, my dear, that if that was the case, he'd have been married to her before now, if I read that woman a-right. As it is, it seems to me that he's got a bit of a job on, keeping the peace, seeing as he works with her. Wouldn't do to fall out with her, would it? I reckon he's trying to keep on good terms with her, because of being with her at the hospital, and trying to protect you, too, and when I was young, if a chap like Dr Ingram protected a young woman, that meant something!'

218

'Don't be silly!' Rachel said shortly. 'Anyway, I've got other worries on my mind. We don't know how Deirdre was affected by that fall. And we don't know if Neil's going to get better.' Reflecting, she added darkly, 'And what is he being so high-handed about Kathy for? If he's got a family who will take her, why didn't they take Felicity?'

'I did hear some talk about that,' Mrs Pym said innocently, considering her gift for listening at key-holes and saying the wrong to get the right. 'Seems her mother was Dr Ingram's favourite sister. Vivian, I did hear her name was. Vivian Ingram – does it ring a bell? No, well, perhaps you don't go to the flicks. I do. I love 'em. She's a film actress. They don't like it, not her family. Perhaps they would if she was a star, but she only plays bit parts, and married the wrong chap. Well, they wouldn't like him, would they, seeing as he was in the film world too? Seems like Dr Ingram's got a bit firm with them all of a sudden,' and she looked at Rachel with bright speculating eyes, in a way that made Rachel colour, and say she was tired, and was going to bed.

Chapter Eight

Rachel's first act the next day was to terminate her employment with Mrs York. 'I'm sorry it had to be like this,' she said. 'I lied to get the job. You didn't know that, did you, but I wasn't married at all.'

Samara looked thoughtfully at her. 'But Dr Fenton said—' she began, puzzled.

'Dr Fenton made things very difficult for me, but of course, my own action gave her plenty of scope. There was a young man of that name – my cousin, actually. A distant cousin. Dr Fenton didn't have to say about him being my husband, but she had her reasons, I suppose,' and Samara York said slowly, 'Yes, she would have those. Well, I'm sorry to see you go, dear, but perhaps it's for the best. What will you do for a living?'

'I don't know,' Rachel said, with a little thrill of apprehension. 'My cousin – the blind one – has … had an accident and is back in hospital. I shall be there with him for a while, until we see how he's going to be.'

'Yes, I saw the ambulance there,' Samara said. 'The neighbours told me … what they heard going on,' she added delicately. 'They were coming to help only that Dr Ingram arrived, so it seemed all right.'

Rachel's colour deepened. That was the worst of a street like Endell Street. There wasn't much that went on that was private. Samara said, 'If I hear of anyone nearby wanting help, shall I mention you, dear?'

She meant it kindly. It was nice to feel one had friends, Rachel thought, as she left the hairdresser's and made her way to the hospital.

Neil was conscious, but practically obscured by bandages. His mouth and ears were uncovered, however, and he had plenty to say. 'Rachel, for heaven's sake tell me – are you *all right?*' So she told him what had happened, and put his mind at rest.

'What a lot we are, for bungling things,' he said at last. 'So we have me in here, in heaven knows what condition. Oh, I'm not in pain, but what will things be like when I come out? And Deirdre – what will she be like?'

'I don't know, Neil, but whether she has to stay in that chair or not,' Rachel said, thinking, 'at least she'll have the thought that she did manage a few steps on her own. She's jubilant about that. I've seen her, and you should just hear her, carrying on about being allowed to try again.'

It didn't do much for Neil, who had guessed that Rachel had given up her job. He was worried about Kathy, too, and didn't like it when he heard that Dr Ingram had Kathy at his own home, with Felicity.

'That's not going to work, you know, Rachel. If things were so difficult there, regarding his own niece and her mother, our Kathy won't help!'

To take his mind off these things, Rachel tried to encourage him to work. 'Would you like to dictate some things for me to type for you, Neil? You know you can trust me with your typewriter.'

He needed a lot of persuading. And it wasn't going to be easy. Most of his work consisted of skilfully weaving together facts and figures from his filing system. Without it, they couldn't work. But Rachel remembered one thing he had been going to do. 'That article about good poetry compared with the sugary stuff on greetings cards.'

'But that depends on me making a few verses myself, Rachel, and I'm not in the mood,' he protested. 'To tell you the truth, I hadn't much hope of ever doing that.'

'Oh, stuff, Neil. You're a *good* journalist. You can write anything. Look, I'll give you a start. Let's see…'

'It has to be about love,' Neil said wryly. He would be thinking about Hazel, Rachel thought wretchedly. But there was no bitterness now. He said, 'Don't worry, I've forgotten Hazel.' Rachel was absurdly pleased.

His little nurse looked in. She was a plain

little thing but she had such a nice smile. In a way, she was Rachel's type. Neil said, 'Is that little Agnes?' and she chuckled.

'You're not to call me that!' she scolded. 'I'll tell Sister!' But she nodded approvingly at Rachel who had got out a pen and pad. Keep Neil occupied, Rachel had been warned, so he couldn't brood and get depressed. Well, his little nurse appeared to have fallen in love with him.

When they were alone again, Rachel said, 'Love, well, yes, I'm hardly an authority on that, but what about this for a start: "I have no gift to give, dear heart. My means are slender, poor." That's mushy enough, isn't it?'

Neil was silent. 'Hey, that's not bad! That's just exactly what I wanted. Yes... How's this to follow? "Someone else may offer you, All I would, and more." And it *rhymes*.' That got a laugh. It was an old joke between them, that the best sentiments wouldn't rhyme, or had too many feet. They settled down to it together.

Rachel was reading out the finished effort to Neil when Boyd Ingram came along. He paused at the slightly open door, shielded by the screen, and listened to her voice. He loved her voice.

'I have no gift to give, dear heart.
My means are slender, poor;

Someone else may offer you
All I would, and more.
  I listen for your footsteps,
  Your voice, your presence dear.
  The uprush of my love for you
  Is so powerful, I fear'

'That's a bit awkward, Neil. Too many feet
there,' Rachel said.

'No, no, go on reading it. Let's hear the
whole thing first!'

'All right,' Rachel agreed, and continued:

'I fear you'll leave me, never knowing
What you mean to me.
Leaving me with fondness growing
And an empty life to be.
  I can't tell you what my heart says.
  Words are not a gift I own.
  Choked I watch you drifting from me,
  Cold, grief-stricken, alone.
What will Fate decree, love, for you?
Chill riches, hollow fame and more?
Or endless glory washing o'er you,
From this loving heart's full store.'

'Now, what do you think?' she asked.

'It really is awful stuff, isn't it?' Neil said,
in a pleased voice. 'You're great guns at it,
Rachel. I tell you what – those lines that had
too many feet in them, we might alter them
by making them mushier. Then we can

quote some Keats and Bryon against it.'

Dr Ingram came into the room. 'Well, you two seem pretty busy. How goes it, Neil?' And to Rachel, 'No, don't go. I want to talk to you both. But first, whose effort was all that? I couldn't help hearing.'

Rachel looked cross. 'Mainly Neil's,' she said shortly.

Neil laughed. 'What a whopper! Mainly Rachel's effort, I'd say.'

Boyd looked pleased to hear Neil laughing. He said, 'Bandages off this afternoon, old son, then we'll see.'

That silenced Neil. Rachel stumbled to her feet. 'Good luck for then, Neil. I'll see if I can come back at tea-time, shall I?' and she went, with determination.

She stood at a window in the corridor below, looking out on to the close-cropped green turf, waiting until her heart stopped thudding, and wondering wretchedly why she had to get into that state whenever Boyd Ingram was near. And what bad luck had brought him unexpectedly into the cubicle just as they were reading that stupid poem about love?

When she had become reasonably calm again, she went to see if she would be allowed to visit Deirdre. Deirdre had a visitor, the man who ran The Gift Shop and took a lot of Deirdre's work.

'Oh, I'll come back again,' Rachel said

225

hastily. 'I thought you'd be alone,' and she smiled at the visitor.

'No, don't go,' Deirdre said. 'You know Hugh Carey, don't you? Hugh, this is my sister Rachel.' It sounded as if Deirdre was singing all that. There was a delicate flush in her cheeks, and she looked so pretty today and her eyes, such an intense blue, shone with something more than happiness. Rachel looked startled, and sought the eyes of the tall man standing by the bed. Hugh Carey very slightly nodded and smiled, and didn't let go of Deirdre's hand. Deirdre beamed at Rachel, their quarrel apparently forgotten.

Deirdre said, 'I told Hugh I managed a few steps. I'm going to try again today. I've been stupid. I mean, what did it matter if I did fall about, in trying? I ought to have kept on. Well, I'm going to!'

'That's right, love,' Rachel said, and kissed her sister.

'No, don't go. I want to tell you something,' Deirdre said. 'Have you heard from Kathy? That nice Dr Ingram has got her at his home with that awful child Felicity. Did you know? Oh, good. Well, of course you would, wouldn't you? Well, he gave me his telephone number to call up Kathy and have a chat with her this morning. Well, I did. I was afraid I'd get his mother on the line – she's awful, they say. Terribly starchy and stiff. But I got the butler and he fetched Kathy, and Kathy was on about going to London with that Dr Fenton after all. Today, she said. You know – to stay at her flat and go to the music school and everything. I thought you said no to all that?'

Hugh Carey, watching Rachel, said quickly, 'I don't think you should bother your sister at the moment, Deirdre, love. She's got enough–'

Rachel cut in, sharply. 'When was this? Are you sure, Deirdre?' and as Deirdre nodded, half frightened, Rachel turned and marched out of the ward.

'Oh, dear, now what have I done?' Deirdre gasped. 'I only wanted her to know–'

Rachel felt the cold hand of fear clutching at her heart. Something bad was going to happen and she couldn't think what. She just had to find Boyd Ingram. She went back to Neil, who was talking to his little nurse. In spite of her anxiety, she noticed how happy and relaxed he seemed.

'Neil, it's me, Rachel again. What happened to Dr Ingram, do you know? Or perhaps you would, Nurse?'

'I think he just went off duty,' the nurse said, looking keenly at Rachel. 'Is anything wrong?'

Neil, full of something that interested him, broke in, 'I say, Rachel, the oddest thing's happened. That poem we did – well, you did, almost all of it – I was going to show Agnes here, and it's gone. She said she saw old Ingram pick up a paper and walk out with it.'

'I expect he thought it was his notes,' Agnes Hersey soothed Neil.

Rachel was hardly listening. 'I must find him. It's about Kathy,' and she didn't stop to listen to what Neil was saying, but hurried away to search for him.

At last, frustrated, she asked someone to bleep him. Her white strained face was enough to convince them that she had to see him. He came over from Residents, looking anxious. 'What is it, Rachel?'

She was furious. 'Deirdre told me she telephoned Kathy. Dr Fenton is taking her to London, to her flat, and to the music school. I told you I wouldn't give my permission for any such thing!'

She had seen him angry before, but never quite like this. He said, 'And I agreed that we wait. Come along, we'll go home and settle this. I was going off duty anyway.'

'Go to your home? But I can't!' Rachel gasped. 'Well, can't you do it on the telephone? I can't go there like this.'

Some of his anger evaporated as he smiled at her, an infinitely tender little smile. 'Oh, Rachel, you delight me. Just when I expect you to be roaring with anger and sweeping everything aside, you go all feminine and fuss about what to wear. I assure you you look very nice, as always. Now come on!' and he hustled her across to the car park.

She didn't know where he would be taking her, but once in his big dark, powerful car, his angry mood settled over him again. She glanced at him and said diffidently, 'Are you going to get furious with Kathy, by any chance, or with Dr Fenton?'

'Probably both,' he said. 'Listen, Rachel, before I went over to Residents, I called in on my old friend, Professor Barnsley, in the Path Lab. He said something to me once about Neil's accident, but it slipped my mind. I remembered it and took him up on it. I've been chasing the wrong idea all along. Although I think we all guessed that Dr Fenton knew more about it than she would admit.'

'You mean there's another witness?' she asked. 'Someone who will admit that it wasn't Neil's and Deirdre's fault?'

'Oh, as to that, I don't think it was a deliberate set-up of witnesses. I don't think for one moment that Dr Fenton would tell strangers to say certain things that weren't true. What I do think might happen is that she possibly suggested to the witnesses, that if they happened to have seen such-and-such, it might just be possible for– Oh, I'm not doing this very well, Rachel.'

'No, you're not,' she said bluntly. 'You're

admitting she perjured the witnesses but you're trying to wrap it up.'

'Rachel, I told you I was going to the newspaper offices. I went with a purpose, to find out who those witnesses were. Well, I did find out. They were patients of hers. Now, human nature being what it is, a witness doesn't always see exactly what happened, and if auto-suggestion is applied especially to patients, who are hoping for something – what I'm trying to say is, they'd try to please their doctor by saying what they thought she'd want, especially if their own memory of what happened was confused, or blurred. Well, that's what I think happened. Not a deliberate lie but a fuzzing of the facts because they were confused.'

'Are you trying to tell me Dr Fenton was in the other car?' Rachel gasped, trying to see where he was leading her. 'And how was it that two patients of hers fortuitously happened to be on the spot?'

'I've discovered that she asked the driver of the other car to give those patients a lift. They were on the spot, unhurt. They had not long been put down, near their homes. Now, this is what I am coming to. I asked my old friend once, if he remembered the accident. He did. I asked him who the other driver was and he said he didn't want to say as I was interested in someone belonging to that person. I thought at the time that that driver was the husband of Mrs Roberts.'

'Mrs Roberts? Why, that's me! Well, what I called myself then.'

'Quite,' he said, and waited, but she obviously hadn't noticed what he had said, about his old friend thinking he was interested in her. So he continued, 'I asked my old friend straight out, today, for the name. He admits he thought at the time that I was interested in Dr Fenton, so he withheld the name of ... her cousin, Max Trent.'

'Max Trent!' Rachel gasped. 'So Neil was right. He kept saying he remembered that voice, something to do with the accident.'

'Max Trent was there, in the car, but he wasn't driving,' Boyd went on. 'My old friend hadn't quite got his facts right. I have since found out, by doing a bit of heavy thinking that I should have done before, that it was his sister Lucille driving. That has been hushed up so much because she's always in trouble for dangerous driving. Thora Fenton told me on the telephone today that she had to go and meet her cousin who was flying in from France, and she sounded very worried. She would be, since, I guess she packed her out of the country indefinitely. She doesn't want her back.'

'Then she isn't going to take Kathy to London if she has to meet—' Rachel began, but Boyd cut in briskly, 'I think she may be doing both.'

Rachel sat sick at heart, conscious of the fear clutching her again, thinking about what Boyd had said. Then suddenly, she said, 'Why did your friend think you were interested in me? Why think the driver was Charlie Roberts?'

He didn't answer. She glanced at him, and something in the glance he turned on her for a moment, made her heart lurch again. There was no reason to suppose it, she told herself, but suddenly she thought she knew why he had haunted their house, until Dr Fenton took it into her head to come with him.

But the fear that clutched her wouldn't go, not even when they arrived at the big stone house that was Boyd's home, and met the cold elderly woman who was his mother. Kathy had gone with Dr Fenton already.

'Why did you let her go, Mother?' Boyd fumed.

'Because you didn't take me into your confidence, my son,' she said evenly and she looked significantly at Boyd's arm, round Rachel's shoulders, and at Rachel's face. 'I have had Felicity here under my roof long enough to come to some conclusion about the situation. Felicity has, for a girl of thirteen, a malicious tongue. I know all about the house in Endell Street and its occupants, and enough about Dr Fenton to come to an apparently erroneous conclusion about your intentions regarding her. Also Dr Fenton herself, in one short visit, to collect Kathy, did her best to make me think you were going to become engaged to her. I take it that it is not so?'

Boyd looked at Rachel. It was all too rushed for her. Up till almost today, she had thought the same about him. He had let Dr Fenton appear to dominate his life. Perhaps, Rachel thought, she didn't really know Boyd. It wasn't enough to love someone, to be hideously unhappy when they weren't around; you had to understand them. In that moment, she thought she understood Boyd. He had deliberately let it appear to anyone who was interested, that Dr Fenton was pushing him around, angling for an official engagement. But Dr Fenton hadn't moved him an inch, because he had been fighting a growing feeling for Rachel herself, whom he had thought was married. And now he at last believed Rachel wasn't married, he was making sure everyone knew whom he was most interested in: Rachel herself. And all without one word of love.

'This,' Boyd said, 'is Rachel Arden,' and he didn't have to say any more. His mother looked at Rachel and said, a little less coldly, 'Then, my dear, if my son introduces you to me in that tone, you and I had better have a little talk. Come with me.'

It was a long day, with the fear still clawing

at her. She talked to Boyd's mother, until that lady had satisfied herself that she knew all about Rachel's side of things. 'Do you love my son?' Boyd's mother asked, at last. Rachel, hands twisting together, thinking of Neil and his eyes, Deirdre and her legs, and Boyd, busy telephoning about Kathy, to-ing and fro-ing to the hospital about the other two, nodded her head without speaking. Boyd's mother said, 'Yes, I believe you do. You and I will do well together, I think. We shall understand each other.'

Rachel flashed her that wonderful smile, and said, 'Forgive me – I'm so distracted. I'm afraid something bad is going to happen.'

'I confess I am not too happy about things myself,' Mrs Ingram said. And then the telephone rang.

It was Boyd, for Rachel. 'Listen, my dear, I have to tell you–' he began.

'Boyd, don't break news to me gently!' Rachel exclaimed. 'Tell me! Is it Neil?'

'No, good heavens, no. That's good news. He can see. No, listen, my dear, I know! It's wonderful news. We did half suspect that the blow on his head might have brought back his sight, but we didn't dare tell you. Listen, it's something else–'

'Deirdre?' Rachel choked.

'No. Good gracious, Deirdre is deliriously happy – she has that chap she sells toys to, haunting the hospital. No, she'll be all right, given time. Given time.'

'Then it's Kathy!' Rachel's voice rose a little, and she went very quiet. Boyd's mother came behind her, and grasped her arm, to give her silent support. She could also hear Boyd's voice, the strong kind of voice that escaped from the receiver.

'No, at least, Kathy wasn't involved. It *is* an accident, but Kathy wasn't with Thora Fenton at the time. She didn't want to go to the airport, it seems. They tell me she pleaded to be taken to the music school and left there, to moon about the place and see what sort of place she'd be blissfully studying in. It's as well she did. I'm afraid it was a bad accident.'

'I suppose you're trying to tell me Dr Fenton was driving,' Rachel said, with difficulty. 'She's dead, isn't she?' and he agreed.

'She was trying to reason with her cousin about something while she was driving,' he said. 'I expect she wanted to send her back to France. Rachel, I know it isn't your worry, but I wanted you to know, because of Kathy. I didn't want you to hear the news until I could tell you what happened. Kathy, of course, will be upset. I'll call and pick you up, and take you to her. Later. There are things I have to see to here...'

'Boyd, you're ... not upset about her, are you? I mean, you didn't care for her all that much, did you?' Rachel asked him.

He said, after a pause. 'She was a colleague. A good doctor. One can't help grieving for a loss like that. But no, not a personal grief. Don't you know who means most to me, in all the world?' and his heart was in his voice.

Rachel said, 'Yes,' because it wasn't the time or the place to make him say her name. That would come, later. She had him to herself now, and their whole lives before them, although it wasn't the way she had wanted it to happen. She said so, to his mother.

'You'll have to face that, my dear. He's in the world of hospital, and he's dedicated. Felicity tells me that your sister was also training to be a nurse, and that she has said if she ever got her legs back, she would return to nursing. That surprises you? Well between the two of them, you'll be in it, you see. My husband, too, was a doctor. These things happen, and life goes on. But you've got a good man, a strong man. My son is a strong man.'

Rachel put her hands to her face, with a little gasp. 'I can't think, it's all happened so quickly. It's such a little while ago since I first met him. He was so shy, he looked afraid of being hurt. But it was all right, once I started talking to him. He *is* strong, isn't he? He'll fix everything up.' She gasped again. 'Yesterday I had nothing, just a great lump of a burden on my shoulders, and now today, I've got everything. Neil's got his sight back, and my sister's going to walk, and Kathy's all right. And there's Boyd...'

'Yes, there's Boyd,' his mother agreed. Felicity's mother, Boyd's sister Vivian, had split the family by her choice of career, and her choice of husband, and Boyd had ranged himself by her, and they had lost him too. She didn't tell this girl. It was too personal, too hurting. But Boyd's mother had much to be happy about now, too. This girl, this Rachel with the winning smile, had brought Boyd back.

The publishers hope that this book has given you enjoyable reading. Large Print Books are especially designed to be as easy to see and hold as possible. If you wish a complete list of our books please ask at your local library or write directly to:

Dales Large Print Books
Magna House, Long Preston,
Skipton, North Yorkshire.
BD23 4ND

This Large Print Book, for people who cannot read normal print, is published under the auspices of

THE ULVERSCROFT FOUNDATION

... we hope you have enjoyed this book. Please think for a moment about those who have worse eyesight than you ... and are unable to even read or enjoy Large Print without great difficulty.

You can help them by sending a donation, large or small, to:

The Ulverscroft Foundation, 1, The Green, Bradgate Road, Anstey, Leicestershire, LE7 7FU, England.
or request a copy of our brochure for more details.

The Foundation will use all donations to assist those people who are visually impaired and need special attention with medical research, diagnosis and treatment.

Thank you very much for your help.